A whisper in ⟨...⟩
could she rea⟨...⟩

Tess shushed it. The man standing before her had devoted hours upon hours of work to fix up the property. The only reason not to trust him at this point was his past, and it wasn't like hers was paved in perfection.

"I think you're underestimating how stubborn Daddy can be. Whatever changes you want to make will be met with resistance."

"I'm sure you're right. We'll do what we can." Sawyer placed his hand on her shoulder, and her nerve endings fizzled. What she wouldn't do to be able to lean into him, let him take charge. "Just try to enjoy the Christmas season. You have a lot to deal with. Leave the ranch to me."

She did have a lot to deal with.

But she couldn't leave it all to him. Wouldn't. Not after Devin.

"Thank you for doing this," she said. "But so we're clear, I'm not going to just leave the ranch to you. I'll still be out there every day, and I expect to be kept in the loop."

Appreciation flashed in his eyes. He took his hand off her shoulder, and she immediately missed the contact. "You have my word."

Jill Kemerer writes novels with love, humor and faith. Besides spoiling her mini dachshund and keeping up with her busy kids, Jill reads stacks of books, lives for her morning coffee and gushes over fluffy animals. She resides in Ohio with her husband and two children. Jill loves connecting with readers, so please visit her website, jillkemerer.com, or contact her at PO Box 2802, Whitehouse, OH 43571.

Books by Jill Kemerer

Love Inspired

Wyoming Ranchers

The Prodigal's Holiday Hope

Wyoming Sweethearts

Her Cowboy Till Christmas
The Cowboy's Secret
The Cowboy's Christmas Blessings
Hers for the Summer

Wyoming Cowboys

The Rancher's Mistletoe Bride
Reunited with the Bull Rider
Wyoming Christmas Quadruplets
His Wyoming Baby Blessing

Visit the Author Profile page
at Harlequin.com for more titles.

The Prodigal's Holiday Hope

Jill Kemerer

LOVE INSPIRED

INSPIRATIONAL ROMANCE

LOVE INSPIRED®
INSPIRATIONAL ROMANCE

ISBN-13: 978-1-335-75887-3

Recycling programs
for this product may
not exist in your area.

The Prodigal's Holiday Hope

This edition published by arrangement with Harlequin Books S.A.

For questions and comments about the quality of this book, please contact us
at CustomerService@Harlequin.com.

Love Inspired
22 Adelaide St. West, 40th Floor
Toronto, Ontario M5H 4E3, Canada
www.Harlequin.com

Printed in U.S.A.

And not only so, but we glory in tribulations also: knowing that tribulation worketh patience; and patience, experience; and experience, hope.

—*Romans* 5:3–4

To Brandon. You missed out on milestone after milestone due to the pandemic, but through it all, you worked hard, stayed strong and never gave up on yourself. I'm proud you're my son, and I'm proud of the man you've become. You have an amazing future waiting for you!

Thank you, Shana Asaro, for the opportunity to write this series and for helping me develop as a writer. I'm grateful for you.

Thank you to Rachel Kent for always believing in my books and for guiding my career. You bless me.

Chapter One

He'd never thought he'd step foot on this land again, yet here he was. The prodigal son had returned. But there was no father welcoming him with open arms, no fatted calf, not even an angry brother to resent him.

Sawyer Roth inhaled the cold Wyoming air and strode along the gravel lane next to the barn where he'd parked. The old farmhouse around the bend hadn't come into view yet. Not quite ready to see it, he slowed his pace and took in the rugged empty landscape surrounding him.

He'd grown up on this ranch. Had worked cattle with his father until graduating from high school and taking off for New York City. When Dad died in a tractor accident a month later, Sawyer had returned for the funeral. Being young and dumb and in love, he'd promptly sold the ranch to Ken McKay. After that? He'd made one mistake after another.

Second chances didn't come around very often, and he'd gladly swallow the remaining speck of his pride to live in Sunrise Bend again. He'd save some cash. Buy a small house on a couple of acres in the middle of nowhere. Be able to hear himself think away from the noise and congestion of the city. The fact Ken McKay was willing to hire him to run the place meant a lot to him.

Sawyer barely registered the snow pellets stinging his cheeks as he continued forward. He wasn't sure how he felt about working the cattle as an employee, but it beat scraping together rent money every month in New York City as a line cook and part-time delivery worker. Thanks to his bumping into a loudmouthed ex-classmate years ago, all of Sunrise Bend surely knew he'd squandered his inheritance in record time.

What they didn't know was why, and he planned on keeping it that way.

He reached the curve in the lane and took a moment to brace himself before gazing in the direction of his childhood home. The white farmhouse looked worse for wear. The paint was chipping, and the roof had dark streaks—a telltale sign it needed to be replaced.

Thirteen years ago, Dad had urged him to reconsider moving to New York City, practically begging him to stay in Sunrise Bend and continue working here.

What would Dad say to him now?

He wouldn't have to say a thing—his disappointment would have been written all over his face.

Movement on the porch caught Sawyer's attention. A woman stood on her tiptoes with a wreath in her hand. Getting in the Christmas spirit early, from the looks of it. She wrestled it onto a hook attached to the door.

He searched his memories for who she could be and came up short. A small boy ran across the porch, and she opened her arms wide right before he launched his little body into them. Her rich laughter carried as she scooped up the toddler and gave him a kiss. A golden Lab had trotted after the boy, and she set the wriggling child down, gave the dog a pat on the head, then turned to take something else out of a cardboard box near her feet.

He'd grown up in this town and didn't recognize her. As he drew near, he got a better look. Large brown eyes under thick eyebrows narrowed as she noticed him. He took in her full lips, high cheekbones, luxurious long brown hair and toned curvy figure. She looked to be in her late twenties. And she definitely wasn't welcoming him.

"May I help you?" Gone was the smile she'd given her boy. In its place? Suspicion. The dog stayed by her side.

"I'm here to speak with Ken McKay." He propped his foot on the bottom step and stared up at her. Man, she was pretty, even if she did seem as bristly as a cornered porcupine.

"I'm afraid that's impossible." She seemed to grow taller as she looked down at him from the porch. Little footsteps pounded across the wooden boards, and the child screeched to a halt beside her.

"Mama, who dat?" The boy, out of breath, pointed to Sawyer.

"It doesn't matter, sweetie." She gathered him close to her leg, keeping her arm around his shoulders. "He's just leaving."

Leaving? He didn't think so. He'd talked to Ken twice last week. The man knew he was arriving today. "This is the McKay ranch."

"Yes."

"Well, Mr. McKay is expecting me. If you'll point me in his direction, I'll be on my way."

She blinked, confusion crossing her beautiful face. "You say he's expecting you. What for?"

"That's between me and him." He had no idea who

this woman was, and he wasn't jeopardizing his new job by spilling information to the wrong person.

"I'm his daughter."

"Oh." *His daughter?* Sawyer hadn't realized Ken had children, but then, why would he? They'd never met. Ken wasn't originally from Sunrise Bend. "When will he be back? Is he on a trip or something?"

"Look, I don't know who you are or what you want, but I think it's best you go."

"I'm Sawyer Roth. The new ranch manager. Your dad hired me last week."

Her cheeks went from pink to red. The vein in her temple pulsed and not in a good way.

"You stay here." Her tone and the way she pointed to him would have made a lesser man squirm. She'd make an intimidating officer, that was for sure. The NYPD should snatch her up. She snapped her fingers to the boy. "Come inside with me a minute, baby."

"But, Mama…"

"No buts. We're checking on Papa."

The little boy and the dog followed her, and they slipped inside. She gave Sawyer a final skeptical glance before shutting the door.

He pivoted to survey the land. Snowy and vast—pure Wyoming. He considered texting Austin Watkins, his best friend from high school who'd told him about the job and badgered him until he'd called Ken. Maybe Austin would know what was going on?

They only talked a few times a year. For more than a decade, Sawyer had avoided every tie to his hometown, but Austin persisted. And Sawyer was glad. Everyone else had given up on him or taken the hint that he didn't want to be in their lives. They'd never know how difficult it had been to lose his father, the ranch and his entire support system in one fell swoop. Of course, all of it had been his fault, but that didn't make it any less devastating.

He tipped his head to the sky and closed his eyes.

Please, God, take pity on me. I'm here with my tail tucked between my legs, fully prepared to eat humble pie for as long as it takes if it means having even a shadow of my life back. I miss this—ranching, silence, fresh air, riding horses, hearing myself think. I can't go back to the city. I just can't do it anymore.

The door swung open, and the daughter stepped onto the faded welcome mat with her arms across her chest, her stance wide.

"You can come in. You've got ten minutes." She looked him up and down as if he'd crawled out of a ditch. "Wash your hands first. I'm timing you. Got it?"

Did he look like a dirty bum or something? Why was he supposed to wash his hands? And why the time limit? Ken had some serious explaining to do. "Yes, ma'am."

She held the door open for him. The dim interior took a moment to get used to. It smelled familiar with an extra dose of cinnamon. The hardwood floors hadn't changed. Still creaked when he reached the middle of the hall leading to the living room, kitchen and dining room. Besides the furniture, the house appeared the same.

A memory of sitting on his mom's lap as she read him a story in front of that fireplace jolted him. How many times had he sprinted into the kitchen for her chocolate chip cookies? She died when he was ten. His memories of her had grown stale, so he pressed this one close to his heart.

"This way." The daughter curtly swished her finger

for him to follow her. She stopped in front of the bathroom. "You can wash up in here."

As he ran the water and soaped up, he studied himself in the mirror. Clean-shaven, short hair, sweatshirt and jeans—nothing said filthy scum in his eyes. He was starting to look old, though. The wrinkles made him look every inch of his thirty-two years. He wiped his hands on the frayed towel and left the room.

She arched an eyebrow suspiciously and took him to the end of the hall. It was the only bedroom on the main floor—his father's room. She knocked with a "We're coming in" and opened the door.

Sawyer took two steps inside. The curtains were drawn. One lamp gave off weak light. Sitting up in bed was a man in his midsixties, scowling. Orange pill bottles lined the dresser. A box of tissues and a glass of water were on the nightstand next to the bed.

"You made it." Ken didn't sound sick, but his hunched shoulders and glazed eyes said otherwise. "Sit down." He pointed to the chair near the bed. Sawyer lowered his lean frame to sit on it. Ken had told him he was retiring. From the looks of it, though, the man was dying. "Don't mind Tess." Ken's cough rumbled deep in his chest. "She's overprotective."

Tess. The name fit her.

"What's going on here?" Sawyer asked. "I'm confused."

"Oh, don't worry. I've got a touch of lung cancer is all. Nothing to fret about. Treatment will be over in a few weeks, and I'll be back to myself."

A touch of lung cancer? Sawyer refrained from commenting. That was like having a touch of the plague. To be fair, if sheer will could overcome the disease, Sawyer had no doubt the old man would conquer it. He had that hardened rancher air about him, much like Sawyer's own father had had.

"In the meantime, you'll be taking over for Bud Delta. He was my part-time ranch hand until the doctors grounded me. He's been running things ever since. He'll show you the ropes the rest of this week, and after that, he'll go back to only working mornings."

Many questions came to mind, but he focused on the most relevant. "Who do I report to? How do you want to handle updates about the herd and state of the ranch?"

"Report to me." He coughed into his fist.

"Uh, how is that going to work? Should I stop by or call you or what?" Sawyer thought of Tess, the militant guardian. How was he supposed to get past her to discuss ranch issues with Ken?

"I'll be out there soon. In the meantime, call me with any problems." A coughing spasm racked his withered frame. Maybe this was too much for him. Now Sawyer understood why Tess had put a time limit on the meeting. "You can get settled in the cabin next to the stables. Keys to it and the outbuildings are on the dresser there."

"Okay. Thanks." He wanted to say something to make him feel better, but tough guys like Ken didn't appreciate sympathy. It would probably be best to pretend nothing was wrong. He had a feeling Ken excelled at pretending nothing was wrong when it came to his health.

Sawyer found the keys and dropped them in his pocket.

"Sawyer?" Ken asked.

"Yes?"

"Don't mess this up. My daughter and grandson are depending on this ranch."

The words sliced through him. As if he needed a reminder his reputation was in shambles. He worked his jaw. For a moment, he wanted to tell him to go ahead and find someone else who would agree to such a low salary. Most cowboys would have laughed in Ken's face at the sum, but what would be the point?

Sawyer needed this job. Needed a little redemption.

Sure, if he'd stayed in New York City, he'd be just another nobody instead of the sum of his mistakes. Being a nobody had its advantages sometimes. And he'd known returning to Sunrise Bend wouldn't be easy. That was why he'd never been back.

It didn't matter what anybody thought of him anymore. He wasn't the dumb kid he'd been at eighteen. He wasn't messing this up. He owed it to his late father to become the man he'd raised him to be.

Had the chemo burned the last of Daddy's brain cells? What on earth would have possessed him to hire that loser to run the ranch? And why hadn't he consulted her first?

Tess Malone paced the length of the living room while Tucker, watching *PAW Patrol*, cuddled with his blankie on the couch. His tiny eyelids drooped. That kid. She'd do anything for him. She'd do anything for her father, too, including keeping the ranch solvent while he was sick.

When Daddy got better, he'd work this land until the day he died. But if he didn't recover? She wouldn't think about it. The man had grit. He'd bounce back. Before long, she'd be arguing with him about the price of hay or buying a new tractor.

He certainly didn't make life easy on her.

Normally, she didn't mind all that much, but hiring

Sawyer Roth? Her blood pressure climbed to the roof. What had he been thinking?

Once again, he hadn't seen fit to inform her of a major decision. Daddy might as well have patted her on the head and told her to go play with her dolls. Didn't he see she was a grown woman? Not to mention, she'd been the one running the financial side of the ranch ever since he was diagnosed with stage-three lung cancer when Tuck was a baby. Shouldn't she have some say in ranch decisions?

She wanted to kick something—the wall, Tucker's stuffed elephant, anything—to release the frustration of dealing with her father.

It wasn't much different from the years of dealing with her husband before they got divorced. Devin had been stubborn and rash and dismissive, too. For years, she'd told him he was spending too much money on the two restaurants he ran for his parents. She'd begged him to cut costs. He never listened. Then, when the bills came in and they couldn't pay them, he'd blame her. The cycle had been exhausting.

It had almost been a relief when she'd caught him cheating on her with Tiffany Snell, one of the restaurants' managers. Almost.

And now Sawyer was in Daddy's bedroom, scheming who knew what. She'd find out soon enough, and by then it would be too late to be the voice of reason.

Her father had no excuse, either. The entire town knew Sawyer had spent every lick of his inheritance within a year of selling this place. One year! How could anyone spend that much money in such a short amount of time?

She let out a half snort. Devin and Sawyer could have been brothers. Her ex had expensive tastes and no discipline. Spoiled. She'd married a spoiled brat.

What a mistake.

Tess's phone alarm chimed. The ten minutes were up. She hoped Daddy hadn't used every remaining ounce of energy in his depleted body. This round of chemotherapy had been tough on him.

As she marched down the hall, her heart pinched. She loved her father. Yes, he annoyed the biscuits out of her, but she loved him fiercely.

Not bothering to knock, she opened the door and almost ran directly into Sawyer's chest. She wasn't expecting the solid wall of muscle. He was around six feet tall. His blue eyes were the color of faded denim. Although wiry thin, strength radiated from him, and it wasn't threatening. It was the kind of strength that made her want to lean into it.

She really did have the worst taste in men.

"Did you get what you wanted?" She tipped her chin up.

His mouth curved slightly. "Yes. I'll be in the cabin by the stables if you need me."

"I won't." She didn't break eye contact as she stepped aside to let him pass. He simply nodded to her and walked away. She waited for the slam of the front door before turning to her father.

"What have you done now?" With her hands on her hips, she glowered at him.

He didn't answer. Just lay back with his eyes closed and hands on his stomach.

"Daddy, what would possess you to hire Sawyer Roth?" She tried to soften her tone, but the words still came out harsh. "He's unreliable. A spendthrift. And who knows what he's been doing since he sold this place to you. I know it hasn't been ranching."

"How do you know that?" His tone told her he was itching for a fight. Well, she was, too.

"Oh, don't play dumb. Dorene Lackey's cousin Bert's son ran into Sawyer in New York City not long after we moved here. He told Bert, who told Dorene, that Sawyer was dirt poor and practically homeless. And Ricky Jennings confirmed his sister saw him bussing tables in a diner the next year. The whole town has known this forever."

"It's none of my business. All I care about is that he knows this ranch like the back of his hand." Daddy sat up a bit and shrugged. "Worked it with his pa. Came recommended to me."

She almost rolled her eyes. "And who exactly recommended him? No one around here has seen or talked to him in years. How did you even find him?" Each question raised a new one. Why wouldn't Daddy hire a local? Why hire anyone at all? Bud had been filling in fine, hadn't he?

"Never you mind how I found him. He has experience and the price was right."

The price. The money. Her blood simmered to a boil. How could she have let that little detail slip?

"You know we can't afford him, Daddy."

"We can't afford not to, Tess." His voice cracked. "It won't be forever. And the cabin is part of his wages."

"How much?" She narrowed her eyes.

"Don't worry about it."

"I have to worry about it."

He glared at her and pointed a bony finger in her direction. "This is still my ranch, and don't you forget it."

"How can I forget it when you refuse to listen to a word of advice I give you?" She shook her head. "Don't think you're going to be riding out there with him anytime soon, either, mister. And I'm not having him coming in here and bothering you while you're on this round of chemo."

"I do what I want." He started coughing.

"Daddy…" Whenever he had a coughing spell, the reality of his poor health drove all other thoughts away. She went to his side. "Are you all right?"

"I'm fine. Got a tickle in my throat, that's all."

"You've got nineteen days left on this round." She took his hand in hers. "Conserve your energy."

"I'm not a fool. I know I'm worthless at the moment." He glanced at her from the corner of his eye. "I'll stick to phone calls with Sawyer for now. I know I can't get out there just yet."

At least he realized his limitations.

He regarded her thoughtfully. "You'll have to go out there in the afternoon when he's back from morning chores. Check on things. Will you do that for me, Tess?"

Daddy was actually asking for her help? This was a first.

"Of course I will."

"I'll be talking to him every day, so don't worry. I've got it handled on my end."

She bent over and kissed his forehead. "I know you do. But if there's a problem, under no circumstances are you going out there to deal with it."

"I love you, Tessie-girl."

"I love you, too, Daddy." She covered him with the blanket. "Need anything while I'm up?"

"No." He sounded tired. She backed away, noting how drawn his cheeks were. These short bursts of energy were usually followed by exhaustion.

"All right. I'll let you rest." She left the room, shutting the door behind her.

If she had her way, she'd boot Sawyer off this land. But she had no authority to fire him. This was Daddy's ranch.

Since he'd asked her to help, though, she'd make good and sure every decision Sawyer made was in their best interests. If she caught him making one wrong move, she'd tell him to pack his bags and never come back.

Sawyer heaved the thrift-store army duffel bag onto the beat-up plaid couch. Dim light from the windows gave the cabin a depressing air. Backtracking to the door, he flicked on the light switch and was relieved to see the entire room illuminated by overhead bulbs.

Home sweet dusty, dirty, cobwebs-everywhere, run-down, musty-smelling home.

A bare-bones kitchen, table for two and living area with a stone fireplace took up most of the limited space. He continued to the back of the cabin, where a bathroom was on the left and across the hall was a small bedroom with a sagging double bed.

The cabin had been built over a hundred years ago out of thick logs. When he was in high school, Sawyer had helped his father replace the roof. At the time, the place seemed no bigger than a closet, but compared to the tight quarters he'd lived in for the past several years, this cabin was a mansion. A little elbow grease would bring the place back to life.

Sawyer returned to the 1989 black-and-silver Ram truck he'd bought last week. He'd been blessed to find one in such good shape for under a thousand dollars. Seemed funny he hadn't owned a vehicle in thirteen years. Hadn't needed one. But now? The truck suited him.

He stacked two large boxes on top of each other and hauled them into the cabin, then repeated the process until all his belongings were inside. For the next couple of hours, he wiped out cabinets, washed grime off every surface, swept, mopped, then cleaned windows. He unloaded the cooler full of food he'd picked up on his way here from a grocery store a town over. Call him a coward, but he wasn't quite ready to face the folks in Sunrise Bend.

After finding bedding in the closet, he gave it a sniff, decided it could use a wash and carried it to the pole barn, where there used to be an old washer and dryer. He hoped the appliances were still there. It took a bit of fiddling with the key ring to find the right one. Then he opened the door and switched on the light.

What a mess. Where his dad's motto had been *a place for everything and everything in its place*, Ken's motto clearly differed. A UTV caked with mud was wedged next to a tractor. A Bobcat with a front loader was parked off to the side. Boxes with parts and packing papers spilling out were strewn across the concrete floor. No matter where he looked, clutter met his eye. And dirt. Lots of dirt.

He could only deal with one thing at a time, and right now he needed to clean the bedding. In the corner under piles of junk stood the old washer and dryer. Sawyer cleared them off, made sure they were still plugged in and started the first load. Thankfully, the washer still worked.

Clicking his tongue, he slowly scrutinized the pole barn. If the main area was in this bad of shape, what did the rest of it look like? Dad had built a series of rooms along the side. A ranch office, a storage room for emergency supplies and a tool closet. Sawyer crossed the space, carefully avoiding the junk along the way, and peered into each of them.

The office looked like any ranch office, so that was good. But the other rooms were disasters piled high with who knew what. He didn't see how anyone could walk through them, let alone find what they needed.

Was the entire ranch this much of a mess?

Things around here were going to have to change.

With slow strides, he returned to his cabin, grabbed a soda from the fridge and collapsed on the couch. His cell phone rang. He glanced at it.

Austin. If it weren't for him, Sawyer would still be flipping pancakes at the diner every morning, delivering takeout every night and barely getting by.

"What's up, man?" Sawyer said.

"Just checking to see if you made it."

"I made it." He hadn't seen his friend in thirteen years, and he missed him. Missed the sense of belonging he'd had with all the guys. Austin, Austin's brother Randy, and Jet, Blaine and Mac. Jet and Blaine were brothers who worked for their father on his ranch east of town. Mac was the son of a wealthy businessman who'd invested in a cattle ranch years ago and given it to Mac to run shortly after Sawyer moved to New York. The six of them had done everything together—football, rodeos, fishing, skiing, hunting, sneaking out at night. As a teen, Sawyer had taken it all for granted.

He'd never take friends for granted again.

"When can we get together?" Austin asked. "I miss you. It's been… Well, I don't know how long it's been, but it feels like a hundred years."

Emotion flooded him, hot and sudden. His throat felt clogged.

"I'm still getting the cabin inhabitable." It wasn't true. The place smelled like lemon-scented cleanser and was officially dirt-free. But he wasn't ready to confront his past. Wasn't ready for Austin to see him as he was now—a washed-up failure.

"The cabin? You don't mean the weekender?" Austin's low chuckle chased Sawyer's embarrassment away, bringing him back to the summer in high school when Dad had gotten tired of the six of them keeping him up all night and had banished them to this cabin, which they'd dubbed the weekender.

"Yep. It's home now." For the moment, anyway. He knew how to live frugally. Living in the little cabin would allow him to save up to buy his own place. A couple of acres would be nice. Nothing fancy. Just a house he could call his own. Something no one could take from him.

Austin let out a low whistle. "Man, the cabin's got to be tight."

"It's not bad," Sawyer said. "You could have warned me Ken had a daughter living here. She wasn't too happy to see me."

"I forget sometimes you don't know everyone here." A moment passed. "Why? Tess giving you a hard time?"

"She didn't know I was coming."

"Typical Ken." He laughed. "Man, those two are as stubborn as they come. They're good people, though, Sawyer. Tess takes care of her dad and is raising that boy on her own. Never misses church."

She did seem loyal. And snarly, like a mountain lion protecting her cubs.

"How about tomorrow night?" Austin asked.

"For what?"

"Getting together. Come out to my ranch. I'll have the guys come out, too."

All of them together like old times. He closed his eyes, regrets washing over him in waves. Old times were good times. But that was all they were—old. He'd changed, and they all knew it even if they hadn't seen him.

Moving back here meant letting people see what he'd become. If he hadn't made such a mess of his life, he might not mind so much.

"I'll have to take a rain check for now."

A moment of silence was followed by a deep exhalation. "All right, for now. But I don't care if I have to rope you and drag you here—we're getting together soon. Jet and Blaine could use a night out. Losing Cody's been weighing on them with the holidays coming."

Austin had called him earlier this year to let him know Jet and Blaine's youngest sibling, Cody, had died in a car accident. Sawyer knew what it was like to lose a loved one in a minute. Austin was right; the holidays would be hard on them.

They spoke a few more minutes before ending the call, and Sawyer tapped his fingertips against his thigh. He'd have to talk to all the guys eventually.

Once upon a time, he'd been a rancher's son like the rest of them. His future had been set.

But a girl named Christina had changed everything.

Within a year of meeting her, he'd lost his father, the ranch, the money and the girl.

He let his head drop back against the cushion and stared up at the ceiling.

In a week or two, he'd get up the guts to meet with his old friends, all of whom were doing well for themselves. Sawyer was glad they were all successful—he just wished he'd made better choices. He wanted to be successful, too.

It wasn't too late for him to turn things around.

Lord, thank You for giving me this opportunity. I might be the hired hand instead of the owner's son, but I'll give this ranch everything I've got. I won't throw away this blessing.

Tess came to mind. Beautiful, self-assured, strong—he couldn't pretend she wasn't his type. She was. And that was why he had to avoid her, or at the very least lock down any feelings she might bring up.

His type of woman had no problem ruining him.

Experience whispered he'd sacrifice anything for a girl he cared about. And when everything was gone and he had nothing left to give, she'd leave him. He'd end up broke and alone. Again.

His life, his needs had to come first. He'd make sure of it. He was ready to reclaim his country roots. One day, one step at a time.

Chapter Two

As far as she was concerned, Sawyer was a city boy in cowboy's clothing. Did he even have the ranching skills Daddy claimed?

Tess buttoned her coat and slipped the baby monitor in her pocket that evening. Her dad had fallen into a deep sleep after supper, and Tucker had conked out more than thirty minutes ago. Ever since Sawyer had arrived, her stomach had been dipping and diving more than the Tilt-A-Whirl she'd ridden at the Wyoming State Fair last summer. As the hours wore on, she'd convinced herself to have a talk with him.

She opened the front door and went outside with their golden Lab, Ladybug, at her heels. Closing the door as quietly as possible, she looked down at the dog. "Well, you ready for this?"

Ladybug wagged her tail and stared at Tess through happy eyes. Oh, to be a dog. Not a care in the world. No trust issues, either. Not with Ladybug, anyway.

"I thought so." Tess braced herself against the cold wind as she hurried down the porch steps to the path leading to the outbuildings. Snow made the lane slippery under her feet. A full moon lit the way and Ladybug ambled by her side.

A curve in the path brought the stables into view. Good, the windows of the cabin glowed. She figured he'd be home since she hadn't heard his truck drive past the house.

What was she going to say to him? She couldn't tell him the truth about their finances. Daddy would never forgive her. But she couldn't let him get away with thinking he could do whatever he wanted to, either. If he was so great at ranching, why had he left all those years ago? Why had he sold this place just days after his dad's funeral?

No, Sawyer Roth wasn't adding up as a good fit here. If she were in charge, she'd fire him, but she wasn't. So the least she could do was warn him that, as the bookkeeper and owner's daughter, she'd be keeping an eagle eye on him.

The cabin porch was up ahead, and she frowned at the three uneven steps leading to it. The place hadn't been used in years. Who knew what kind of shape it was in? The last time she'd been in here, it had been full of dust, cobwebs and probably mice. For a moment, guilt hit her that it hadn't been cleaned. He was likely ornerier than a nest of wasps at having to deal with the mess.

After taking off her mittens, she knocked sharply on the door. The bumps of approaching footsteps reached her ears. Then Sawyer filled the door frame with light glowing behind him.

"Oh, hi." He looked taken aback.

"Can I come in?" she asked. Ladybug stood by her feet. "Do you mind my dog?"

"I like dogs." He stepped aside for her to enter, then gestured to the couch and chair. "Have a seat."

Her jaw almost fell to the floor. The cabin had been spit shined within an inch of its life. It smelled good, too. Where before it had been derelict and creepy, it was positively homey now.

"Wow, you've been busy. Sorry about it being such a mess." Embarrassment blasted her cheeks as she sat in the chair. "I would have cleaned, but…"

"You didn't know your father hired me." His lips flashed into a kind smile. "Don't worry about it. It felt good to get the old cabin in shape. What's your dog's name?"

He wasn't mad? She couldn't imagine he was the type to find satisfaction in cleaning the place. But she'd be the first to admit she only knew him by his reputation.

"Her name's Ladybug." The dog made a beeline to Sawyer, who'd plunked his lanky frame onto the couch. The Lab, waiting patiently to be petted, sat in front of him, tongue lolling.

Sawyer beamed as he scratched behind the dog's ears. "You're a good girl, aren't you?" Ladybug, naturally, ate up the affection.

The moment grew awkward as she tried to form an impression meshing Mr. Clean here with a worthless spendthrift. Things weren't adding up. But she'd been in his presence for all of two minutes, so what did she know?

"You must love Christmas." He glanced her way.

"What?"

"The wreath and lights. You were decorating the porch. Thanksgiving is still two weeks away, so I figure you must have a thing for Christmas, to be decorating this early."

She'd never thought of herself as having a thing for Christmas, but it was probably true. The holiday never ceased to fill her with wonder. This year held an extra urgency with Daddy's health being so poor. She wanted it to be as Christmassy as possible for him. After all, it could be his last.

She gulped. "I mostly wanted to get started before the weather turns too cold."

"Ah."

"I'll be keeping an eye on things for my father over the next couple of weeks." It was high time she reminded herself she wasn't here for a neighborly chitchat. "He's wrapping up this chemo cycle and has to rest."

"Chemo, huh?" His eyes warmed with compassion. "I'm sorry. It must be hard seeing him so ill." The empathy in his tone surprised her.

"Thank you." She swallowed sudden emotions. It *was* hard seeing her tough-as-nails father bedridden. "You'll likely be getting a lot of calls and texts from him, but with his immune system so compromised, I've got to keep him isolated. So, if there's any serious concerns or issues, bring them to me."

"How bad is it?" His gaze locked with hers, and her lungs squeezed. Man, this guy seemed sincere. And those blue eyes were as inviting as the hot springs a few hours west of here.

"It's fine. He'll be fine," she said quickly. "Doesn't like being stuck inside, mind you, but he understands."

It was on the tip of her tongue to warn him his job would be short-lived. Either Daddy would get better and run the ranch himself or...

It was hard to think of him dying. If the worst happened, she'd have to make some tough choices. She didn't have the trust levels to hire someone else to manage the place, but she couldn't stand the thought of selling it, either.

Maybe that was why Daddy had hired Sawyer. He was worried about the ranch continuing in the event he didn't make it.

This ranch was home, and there wasn't a better place to raise her son. But the money… Just thinking about how they were going to come up with the cash to pay Sawyer sent invisible hands around her throat.

"Look, I know you grew up here. I've been told you have experience." She tried to keep the disdain out of her tone but didn't quite succeed. Arching her eyebrows, she leveled a stare his way. "I've also been told other things."

"What did you hear?" It was his turn to stare her down. He didn't seem angry or upset, merely curious.

"I heard you've been living in New York City, and after you sold Daddy the ranch, you spent your way through your entire inheritance in no time flat. Rumor has it you were working at a diner and living in a rough neighborhood."

"I see." His throat worked, but he didn't look away. "Is that all?"

"No." She watched him carefully. "I don't have a problem with honest work. But why? You had the money from the sale of the ranch. Unless… Well, some say you had a gambling problem or a drug addiction—maybe both."

"Some always have a lot to say, don't they?" He shrugged.

"Yeah, *some* do."

He turned his attention to scratching Ladybug's neck. "They got a few parts wrong."

"What parts?" The hair on her arms rose. She hoped they were wrong about the gambling and the drugs. If not, she'd kick him out whether Daddy approved or not. For her son's sake.

"I did move to the city. My inheritance was gone in no time flat. I worked at a diner—and plenty of other low-paying jobs—to survive. My home for going on thirteen years was in a safe, affordable neighborhood. I have a few pennies to my name. Not many, but a few."

"And the rest?"

He shrugged. "People believe what they want to believe."

"You're not denying it."

"If I did, would it matter?"

"It would matter to me."

"Then, no, I've never had a gambling problem, or a drug addiction, for that matter. I don't gamble or do drugs."

She was inclined to believe him, but… "How could you have spent all that money, then?"

"My life isn't an open book." The transparency in his eyes closed abruptly. "Some secrets are mine to keep."

Fair enough. She didn't like it, but she understood. She had her own shameful moments she preferred to keep to herself.

"Just so we're clear, this ranch means everything to my father. I'm not going to let him lose it for trusting the wrong person."

His head tilted as he regarded her. What did he see?

She shivered. Could he feel the resentment she'd bottled up toward her ex-husband? Could he sense the failure permeating her for being blind to his affair? The self-loathing for allowing him to override every decision she'd suggested? The anger that he and his parents had cut Tucker out of their lives as if the boy didn't exist?

Did he have any idea how terrified she was that she was going to lose Daddy and her home, as well?

"This ranch means something to me, too." His voice was low and gravelly, and it made her heart beat faster.

The wood in the fireplace popped and crackled, the same as her nerves. A muffled sound came from the baby monitor. She'd better get back.

"I'm warning you now—Daddy is going to drive you batty calling for updates. If there's anything that needs immediate attention, call me."

"I will. What's your cell number?" He crossed over to the kitchen counter and swiped his phone. She told it to him and stood, heading to the door with Ladybug joining her. Seconds later, her phone chimed.

"I'm going back, but I'll be around, keeping an eye on things."

One side of his mouth quirked up and his dancing eyes clearly found her amusing. She let out a humph and turned to leave with Ladybug by her side. "Good night."

"Good night, Tess." He opened the door for her. "By the way, what's your last name?"

"Malone." Shivering, she made her way straight down the porch without looking back.

Tess Malone. Stupidest thing she'd ever done was marry Devin. If the divorce had taught her anything, it was to stand up for herself. She'd given up way too much of her power over the years. From here on out, she'd make better decisions with the good Lord by her side.

The biting wind was a rude reminder of how bleak Wyoming could be in the winter. Sawyer's fingers were frozen inside the leather gloves the following morning, but he pressed on with Bud Delta at his side. They'd fed the cattle earlier and broken the ice covering the water tanks. Now they were checking the remaining cows before heading back.

Sawyer wasn't entirely surprised at the run-down appearance of everything. The cabin and pole barn hadn't been isolated cases of neglect. The entire ranch needed a healthy dose of TLC.

Maybe the miserable weather was giving him gray-colored lenses or something, but he found the ranch depressing. Entire sections of fence were in need of obvious repairs, the watering tanks were in poor condition, the equipment in the sheds was stored haphazardly and the outbuildings had missing shingles and peeling paint.

This place needed a lot of work.

Sawyer didn't mind hard work. Even as a little kid, he'd ridden out with his father and helped maintain the ranch. He'd been taught to do things right the first time. They'd always kept up with regular maintenance to prevent bigger problems.

Why had Ken allowed everything to deteriorate?

"We're pert near done." Bud, a heavy man in his late fifties with a long gray beard, turned his horse back toward the ranch. He'd complained all morning about the icy weather, his aching joints and the dumb cows. He seemed to be under the impression he was the one in charge, while Sawyer had been hired to be the ranch hand. Sawyer decided to get a feel for the operation before setting the man straight.

"Looks like we missed a couple." Sawyer pointed to a group of black cows in the distance. Bud gave him a long glare.

"You go ahead and check 'em. I'm going back." The

man didn't hesitate in heading the opposite way. Sawyer moved forward on his own.

As he approached, the cattle looked up at him and chewed foraged vegetation. He was glad they weren't skittish. They didn't seem to consider him a threat. After looking them over, he made one last sweep of the pasture, then signaled his horse to turn back.

All morning he'd been trying to get Tess's visit from last night off his mind, and all morning he'd failed. There was something about her. Something direct and unapologetic. Sassy, even.

He didn't blame her for being skeptical of him or for believing the rumors she'd heard. Small towns like Sunrise Bend spread gossip faster than a prairie fire during a drought. There were probably other unsavory stories circulating about him, too, and he didn't need to know them nor did he care. Only a few people's opinions about him mattered. Bridget Renna, his friend in New York who was practically his little sister, and his buddies from high school.

What would the guys think when he finally got the guts to meet with them?

He'd find out soon enough, he supposed. As for Bridget, he'd tried to convince her to move out here, too, but she'd been hired to manage a high-end coffee shop back in New York. She didn't want to leave the city, the only home she'd ever known. She'd loved hearing about Wyoming, though, and hung on his tales of growing up in Sunrise Bend. Although not blood-related, they were the only family each other had. Bridget had been in similar straits as he—broke, homeless, alone—when they'd met. Last night, he'd talked to her, and the conversation had improved his mood.

Life would be easier if he was attracted to someone

mellow like Bridget. But, no, he always gravitated to the strong-willed ones. Like Tess.

As he made his way back to the stables, Sawyer kept his eye out for other potential problems. By the time he arrived, he was more than ready to get out of the wind and warm his hands. He unsaddled his horse, rubbed him down and led him out to the corral with the rest of the horses.

Washing his hands under warm water, Sawyer felt his fingertips tingle back to life. Now what?

A hot list.

He needed some paper and a pen. He ventured to the doorway of the office. Ken's domain, from the looks of it. A long-forgotten coffee tumbler was covered in a fine layer of dust next to a yellow legal pad with several pages flipped over. Trade journals, a telephone, pens and a stack of manila folders bursting with papers tottered on the desk. A folding chair sat in the corner. Last year's calendar had been pinned on the wall with a thumbtack.

Sawyer borrowed the legal pad, carefully tearing off the used pages and setting them on top of the manila folders. Then he poured out the to-do list he'd been mentally tallying all morning.

When he couldn't think of anything more to add, he circuited through the building, jotting down the action items, including organizing the tool and supply rooms and cleaning up the main area.

Did Sawyer need permission to organize this place?

He debated calling Ken. The man was really sick, and he probably shouldn't disturb him. But then again, Ken had texted him three times today already to ask about the cattle.

Maybe he should ask Tess.

He hadn't seen her yet. She'd said she'd be around, keeping an eye on things. Watching and waiting for him to mess up was more like it.

Sawyer ran his hand down his cheek. Ken had hired him to manage the place and that included the buildings. But what if he resented Sawyer moving things around?

Lord, I need some help here. You brought me back home for a reason. Dad would hate to see the ranch in this state. Do I clean it up? Organize it? Do I ask permission? Do I even need permission?

One of the garage doors opened, and Bud drove the UTV inside, parking it in the previous grooves of caked mud on the floor. He heaved his bulky frame out of it, took off his gloves and blew on his hands.

"Oh, good, you're back." Sawyer scanned the list he'd been making. "I've got some questions." He moved his index finger down the paper until he found the section marked *urgent*. "How much hay do we have on hand?"

"I dunno." Bud shrugged, his expression darkening.

"I need you to find out. Can you estimate it?"

"It's behind the barn for anyone to see." His arrogant gaze sharpened.

Hold your cool. Not worth getting into it on your first day.

"How are you keeping track of the pregnant cows?" Sawyer tapped the pen against the legal pad.

"Ask Ken." Bud crossed his arms over his chest and widened his stance. The guy wasn't real forthcoming.

"What are all these boxes and parts for?" Sawyer pointed around to the various boxes on the floor.

"Fixin' stuff. I don't know. Look, it's lunchtime. This ain't my problem." Bud turned to leave, muttering under his breath, "Worse than the daughter. Comin' out here, yappin' about nonsense. No wonder her husband left her..."

"Excuse me?" Sawyer straightened, setting the legal pad on top of a box. "What did you say?"

Bud pivoted then and glared at him. "I said you're worse than Ken's daughter. I don't blame her ex for leaving her for another woman. Serves her right the guy knocked up his girlfriend."

In three strides, Sawyer was in his face. "Let's get something straight. You will respect your boss and his daughter. I was hired to manage this ranch, and I don't want to hear another word about her out of your mouth. Got it?"

"Oh, you're the manager, huh?" Bud let out a derisive laugh, spittle falling on his beard. "You might think you're running the show, but everyone in this town knows you're dumb as a box of rocks. So, why don't *you* get something straight. I'll say whatever I want about Ken's uppity daughter, and you don't tell me what to do."

Sawyer took a deep breath, trying to hold in his temper and failing. He clenched his fists down by his thighs.

Bud hitched his chin. "Now I'm going to go eat lunch, and when I get back, I'm checking on the steers like I've been doing every afternoon Ken's been gone. You want to know how much hay we have? Figure it out yourself." He stepped closer to Sawyer and looked in his eyes. "You got that, Mr. Manager?"

The man lumbered away, and Sawyer ground his teeth as he watched him go.

Bud was the only other employee Ken had, and for the ranch's sake, they needed to have a good working relationship. He didn't care if Bud thought he was a joke, but he refused to listen to anyone disrespecting his boss or the boss's family. It wasn't right.

He should have told Bud off. He should have put him in his place. He should have…

Sawyer flung open the door to the toolroom. He didn't need permission to organize it. Ken had cancer. Bud had an attitude problem. They all thought he was dumb as a box of rocks? Fine. He might have sold the ranch and lost his inheritance, but he wasn't the one who had done such a rotten job of taking care of this place in the years since.

He was getting it back in shape. Starting today.

Later on, he'd call Ken and go through the list of urgent ranch matters, but he'd deal with Bud on his own. He hadn't gotten up the courage to come back here to let a guy like Bud push him around.

For the first time since arriving, Sawyer finally felt like he'd made it home.

Daddy's cell phone rang as Tess wiped his forehead with a damp washcloth later that afternoon. He'd been having a hard day. She'd heard him vomiting earlier. After a few sips of Pedialyte, he fell back against his pillow, his face pale and slack. She teased him about her cooking not being *that* bad, and he hadn't even had the energy to joke about the chicken soup she'd left for him.

Her heart squeezed every time she witnessed him suffering. How much more could his body take?

At this rate, she didn't know if he'd make it to Christmas.

Fear clutched her chest. She wanted to scream that it wasn't fair. Wanted to strangle the disease stealing her father. Watching him suffer left her helpless.

Come on. Don't let him see you worrying.

The phone kept ringing. Sawyer's name was on the screen. "It's Sawyer. Want me to tell him to call you back later?"

He closed his eyes and nodded. She picked up his phone and padded out of the room.

"I'm sorry, but Daddy's not up to talking right now," she said, her stride lengthening in the hallway. "Can you call back in the morning?"

"I'm sorry to hear that, Tess." His low voice did sound sorry, too. "I have a list of things to run by him, but they can wait. Sorry to trouble you."

"You didn't." At the sympathy pouring through the line, her muscles relaxed. The ranch didn't stop just because her father was sick. If she could lighten his load by dealing with Sawyer's list, she would. "Why don't you run it by me?"

His hesitation positively crackled through the line. "Are you sure?"

She stiffened as she neared the kitchen. Was he implying she couldn't handle his list?

"Yes."

"If you need to take care of your boy, I understand."

Well, those weren't the words she'd expected. "Tucker. His name's Tucker. And he's playing with cars on the floor at the moment, so I'm all yours." She cringed. Why had she said the last part? She was not all his. She was her own, and that was the way it would stay.

He cleared his throat. "Okay. You don't happen to know how much hay you're storing, do you?"

"No. I can find out how much seed we bought and how much hay we had to purchase last year, but I don't know how much we currently have on hand." She sat on a bar stool at the counter where she could keep an eye on Tucker.

"That's okay. I'll poke around the stockpile and try to estimate it. Do you recall the number of pregnant cows you have? Bud doesn't know, and I can't find any records."

"I don't." Frowning, she realized how little she knew about the practical matters of the ranch. It wasn't as if she hadn't ridden out with Daddy often throughout the years, but she hadn't exactly picked up his expertise. She did track every dollar of income and every expenditure, though.

"No problem," he said. "I hope this doesn't come off wrong, but the outbuildings are rather unorganized."

"That's an understatement. Daddy claims he has a system. If a tornado touched down on the pole barn tomorrow, it would be improved."

His laugh shot straight to her core. It was deep, hearty and stirred a longing inside her. It had been a long time since she'd laughed in easy companionship with a man. She missed it.

"Do you think Ken will mind if I put things back in order?"

"Be my guest." Every time she went to the stables, sheds or the pole barn, the same thing greeted her. Piles of junk. And it gave her a headache. It had taken her two months to get the books in order. She simply didn't have the energy or desire to tackle the rest of the ranch.

"Good, because I already started."

It was her turn to laugh. "You don't waste time, do you?"

"I've wasted enough time."

The words sobered her. She could say the same about

herself. Even now, her life wasn't really her own. She'd never planned on living here again, but shortly after the divorce, Daddy got his cancer diagnosis. The logical thing to do was move in with him. She'd have a place to stay, and her father would have someone taking care of him. It was a good thing she had, too, since his health took a nosedive over the summer. She'd been caring for him, raising Tucker and trying to keep the ranch afloat for going on two years.

Helping her father was a privilege, but it also brought a lot of responsibility. She'd had many sleepless nights trying to figure out how to keep it all together. Sometimes she longed to rent an apartment in town, find a job and leave her father's messes behind.

Like that would ever happen—she'd do anything for Daddy.

"What else you got?" she asked.

He went down a line of proposed improvements. Most could be done without spending a dime, and for that she was thankful. At least he wasn't coming in here with expensive suggestions to fix up the place.

"There's a storm forecasted later this week," Sawyer said. "I noticed some of the fences need repairing. I'll get as much done as I can before the weather hits."

"Bud should be able to help with that." Bud had been Daddy's ranch hand for a while now. She didn't like the guy much, but her father seemed to be okay with him. And Daddy had never been afraid of hard work. He did the work of three men easily. He used to, anyway.

"Tell Ken I'm taking care of everything and not to worry."

"I will." How twenty-four hours had changed things. Yesterday, she would have made a snarky comeback at his claim of taking care of everything, but after seeing how well he'd cleaned up the cabin, she was inclined to trust him on this.

"Thanks for the talk," he said. "Have a good night."

The line went dead with the words *thank you* on her tongue.

Surprise, surprise. Maybe Daddy's hire hadn't been the mistake of the century after all.

She rolled her eyes, shaking her head. It had only been one day.

No matter how much Sawyer cleaned and organized the ranch, it wouldn't bring in the cash so desperately needed. At least he had one thing going for him—he was earning his keep.

Chapter Three

She owed Sawyer an explanation.

Tess carried a container filled with leftovers down the lane to his cabin with Ladybug leading the way. She hated to do this on Thanksgiving. Well, she hated to do it at all, but the past two weeks had convinced her Sawyer deserved to know that come January they would not be able to pay his salary.

It wasn't fair to leave him under the impression this was a long-term gig. He'd been working his fingers to the bone to get the ranch into some sort of order, and Tess had seen it for herself. Every afternoon, she brought Tucker to the pole barn, where Sawyer would be slogging through one of the storage rooms. He'd take a break to update her on the cattle, and she'd slowly been learning more about him as they chitchatted.

He loved being outdoors, had kept his body fit in New York by walking everywhere. He preferred to reuse things rather than buy new, and he had more patience than anyone she'd ever met.

His interactions with Tucker proved it.

Every afternoon, Tuck begged to sit on the tractor

and pretend to drive. And every day, Sawyer, bless his heart, would swing her son onto the tractor with him. The kid ate it up. He'd taken to calling the tractor *twac, twac*. It was cute.

Tess shivered against the cold as she picked her way across the icy gravel. Sometimes Sawyer seemed too good to be true.

No one was too good to be true.

Everyone had flaws. Some more pronounced than others.

Was she doing the right thing? Telling Sawyer about the ranch's finances, or lack thereof, was a risk in more ways than one. Daddy wouldn't like it. And Sawyer might quit. If her father would just listen to her about improving their cash flow… But he wouldn't. He loved her, but he did things his way. Always had.

At least Daddy was getting his strength back. He eagerly anticipated every call from Sawyer. Part of his improving health was surely due to talking shop with Sawyer every day.

She stumbled over a rock in the path. *Watch yourself.* That was what she got for having her head in la-la land.

Gripping the container tighter, she firmed her steps. Smoke curled out of the chimney of the log cabin, a cheery scene surrounded by snow-topped pines. The sun was starting to set, so she forced herself to pick up her pace. After a few swipes of her boots on the welcome mat, she shifted the container and knocked on the door.

Sawyer opened it, his face screwing up in confusion. "Is something wrong?"

"No, nothing at all." Well, a lot in her life was wrong, actually, but… "I thought you might like some leftovers. You should have eaten with us. We had too much food."

She hadn't seen his truck leave all day, nor had anyone driven here. On more than one occasion, she'd asked him to spend the holiday with them, but he'd declined. And he'd clearly spent Thanksgiving alone. Sadness pricked her heart.

"Here, let me help with that." He took the box out of her hands and stepped back as Ladybug surged inside and made herself at home on the rug. "Come in."

She toed off her boots and took off her coat while he set the box on the counter. A small Christmas tree—freshly cut, from the smell of it—stood in the corner. It wasn't decorated yet.

"You got a tree," she said.

"Yeah, I cut it down this morning. I saw it when I was riding along the creek. Didn't think you'd mind."

"I don't. Not at all. It looks nice." She crossed over to the couch and took a seat. Two days ago, she'd set up a Christmas tree. Tucker had loved helping decorate it even when he'd gotten sidetracked by the candy canes. She was glad he was old enough to start making their own holiday traditions together. "Happy Thanksgiving, by the way."

"Happy Thanksgiving." He sat in the chair adjacent to her. Neither spoke. The moment grew awkward.

"Did you do anything special today?" she asked. Questions she hadn't asked him came to mind. What did he think about living in Wyoming again? Was it weird being an employee on the ranch he grew up on? How had he spent all the money from selling this ranch in such a short amount of time? Did he have a girlfriend?

She shushed the questions, especially the last two. Those were none of her business.

"Not really," he said. "The cattle are all doing well. They don't mind the snow."

The cattle? What about family and friends and celebrating a good meal together? "I'm sure it can't be easy being away from your life in New York this holiday season."

His blue eyes twinkled. "I don't miss New York. I miss Bridget, but we talk every day on the phone, so it's not so bad."

Bridget? Her teeth scraped together. In their afternoon getting-to-know-you sessions, that name hadn't come up.

"I keep trying to convince her to move out here, but she grew up in the city." His face was open, relaxed, and his grin chased away the chill. "She's my little sister. Not in blood, but in spirit."

His little sister. Not related.

Relief flowed down her spine. How did that work? Who cared? It seemed to be platonic. She leaned back and crossed one leg over the other.

"How old is she?" she asked.

"Twenty-five." The pride in his voice rang through clearly. "She helped convince me to return to my roots."

"Has it been hard? You know, working here when it used to be yours?"

"Not really. Mostly, it's just nice to be back."

"You're doing a good job here. I can actually walk through the pole barn without tripping over anything. And I honestly never knew the toolroom was a toolroom. I thought it was where everyone threw their junk."

He lowered his gaze and shrugged. "I've got a long way to go, but I promise you I'll have this place in top shape come spring."

It would be so easy to not say another word. To let Daddy deal with the consequences of his decisions. But she didn't have it in her. She had to tell him the truth.

And she didn't want to.

How many times had she been in a similar position with her ex-husband? Dreading showing him the restaurants' unpaid bills, begging him to cut back on expenses. Knowing he'd dismiss her at first. Then when crunch time came, he'd blame her for his ridiculous purchases until he'd finally assert his authority and announce the restaurants were his to run. He had the final say. End of story.

He was right, of course. His parents technically owned the franchises even if Devin ran them. But the income fed her family, and she'd worked hard to keep them profitable. Devin hadn't given her any credit.

And here she was again, stuck being the bearer of bad news not of her making.

"Yeah, about spring…" She averted her gaze. She'd prayed about this. If she were in his shoes, she'd want to know the ranch was bleeding money. "I'm going to be straight with you. Money's tight."

"How tight?" His eyebrows furrowed together as he leaned forward.

"Tighter than my jeans after two slices of pumpkin pie and a mound of whipped cream." She spoke from experience. She shouldn't have gone for round two so soon after supper.

His lips quirked up. "You look good to me."

The compliment rushed through her, sending warmth to her cheeks. She glanced at him. His face had grown red. For some reason, that made her feel better.

"If you haven't noticed, my father is as stubborn as they come. There's not much I can do about the financial situation. He doesn't listen to me."

"Why are you telling me this?"

"Come January, I have no idea how he'll pay you." There. She'd said it.

He slumped back, pursing his lips as he considered her words. "What do you think he'll do? Fire me?"

"No. He wouldn't have hired you knowing you were moving across the country just to let you go."

"You say he doesn't listen to you." Sawyer watched her. "What would you advise him if he did?"

This was a new one. Someone actually wanting her opinion?

"I've told him to consider cashing in one of his retirement investments. I've also mentioned selling a parcel of land. There are three he could sell to one of the neighbors."

Sawyer nodded. "Neither of those solve the problem, though."

Disappointment blew through her with a swoosh. As usual, her ideas were shot down.

"Investments and land run out eventually," he said. "I get where you're coming from, though. Either option would free up cash. You're not a partner or anything with your dad, correct?"

"I am not." She'd been using the child support she received from Devin to help pay the household expenses, and she gladly did the ranch's bookkeeping for free, but she had no stake in it other than being her father's sole heir.

"If you were in charge, what would you suggest as a long-term plan?"

She blinked. Was this a trick question? "Cutting costs."

"I might be able to help you with that." He nodded thoughtfully.

"What did you have in mind?"

"I've been here long enough to see how things are done." Sawyer debated the wisdom of having this conversation, but Tess's honesty overrode his reservations. Getting to know her bit by bit every afternoon had given him a whole new respect for the single mom. She was savvy, smart and cared about the ranch's success. "I've already reduced feed waste."

"Feed waste?" Her pretty dark eyes met his. "Is that why you're keeping those spreadsheets?"

"Yes. I started measuring the hay we roll out every day. Then I go back to see how much is left once the cattle have eaten. It's helped me get a better idea of how much hay they really need."

"Were you seeing a lot of waste?"

"Yes." He saw no point in lying to her.

"I'm surprised Bud allowed it." She drummed her fingers on the arm of the couch. "What else?"

"I've had time to evaluate the land, and it looks to me like you're under-producing hay. You had to supplement last year, right?"

"Yes, we bought additional hay from Tolbert Ranch."

Tolbert Ranch—Sawyer knew it well. His high school buddy Mac Tolbert owned it. His conscience pinched. For two weeks now, he'd avoided Austin's attempts at getting together with him and the guys. Hadn't taken any of their calls, either. Stupid pride. He needed to bite the bullet and get it over with soon. Whatever they thought of him couldn't be worse than what he'd thought of himself over the years.

"The north pasture is a hostile growing environment for crops, but there are grass seed mixtures we can plant that will thrive." He could envision it next summer. "It would help supplement the feed."

"But that won't help with costs until next year. And

cutting back on wasted hay doesn't bring in income today."

He couldn't argue with her. However, if the ranch were his, he'd do whatever it took to get it profitable ASAP. He knew plenty of ways to bring in money *and* cut costs.

Tess looked pale and tired. She usually had a vitality about her drawing him to her like the cattle to their morning meal.

"You're really worried about this place, aren't you?" he asked.

Startled, she jerked to attention. "It's home."

It was home. For him, too.

"It's everything to Daddy." She swiped her hair behind her ear. "Ever since you arrived, he's got more life in him. He looks forward to your calls every day. He's chattering about calving in the spring and how he needs to check the fences in one of the pastures. You help take his mind off his condition."

Sawyer tended to forget Ken had cancer. He hadn't seen him since the day he'd arrived. Surprisingly, he looked forward to their daily calls, even when Ken disagreed with him or got his temper riled up over one of Sawyer's suggestions. It reminded him of talking to his father.

It had been a long time since Sawyer had dealt with a Wyoming rancher similar to his dad, and this time around he had a lot more patience.

"How is he doing? His health and all?"

A smile danced on her lips, lighting her eyes. "Oh, he's sicker than a dog most days, but you'd never know it. Like I said, your daily phone calls have breathed new life in him. I hope you're not offended at how gruff and unreasonable he can be."

He chuckled. "Reminds me of my own dad. I can handle it."

Her happy expression melted away. He got the impression life was weighing heavy on her. She was probably terrified of losing Ken.

What would happen to this place if he died? If the cash situation was as dire as she claimed, Tess would have to sell the ranch, wouldn't she?

Sawyer's lungs hollowed out. Working here, even for such a short time, had forced him to admit what he'd ignored for the past dozen years.

Ranching was a part of him, the same as his blue eyes and the scar on his right knee from falling onto a jagged rock when he was eight.

He'd moved here banking on the fact he'd have a job for the long haul. He'd crunched the numbers and, even with his small salary, figured it would take eighteen months to save enough for a down payment on a house nearby with a few acres.

His days would be filled with hard work. He'd have privacy. A life he could be proud of. And now it was being threatened.

"Did *you* come over today to fire me?" he asked.

"No!" Her mouth dropped open in horror. "Of course not. I should have told you all this the day you arrived, but it wasn't my place. It isn't my place." She sighed. "It just didn't seem right to let you keep working so hard without knowing what's coming. Especially with Christmas right around the corner."

A layer of sadness rested on her pretty features. While he liked the fact her emotions were easy to read, he wished she could enjoy life a little. But who was he to talk?

She wrapped her palms around the back of her neck and looked up at the ceiling. "Daddy isn't one to discuss his plans, but I imagine he'll ask both you and Bud to work part-time in January if he feels better."

Sawyer didn't like Bud much, but he was doing his best to get along with the guy. Every chore Bud handled, Sawyer ended up having to go back and finish it right. It wasn't that the man didn't do what was expected—he did, but with minimum effort. Taking care of a ranch this size was too hard for one cowboy alone, so Sawyer had been putting up with it.

The smart thing to do would be to find out what other jobs were available in the area. But one glance at Tess and he knew he wouldn't be doing the smart thing anytime soon.

Deep in thought, with her forehead wrinkled, she nibbled on her fingernail.

Sympathy and the unbearable need to fix things pressed on his chest. He knew how to ease Tess's burdens, but—

No. It would be a mistake. Look at how Christina had taken advantage of him. He couldn't leave himself vulnerable like that again.

"Well, I should go." Tess stood and smiled at him. It was full of warmth and regret.

"What's going to happen to you?" He rose.

"What do you mean?"

"If the ranch can't pay its bills, will you and Tucker be okay?"

"Don't worry about us. It's high time I figured out a way to support myself anyhow. I'll come up with something."

He was no stranger to tight finances, and they always seemed worse this time of the year. Christmas was his favorite season. He always had to work on the holidays, but the day after Christmas, he and Bridget would order a pizza and exchange presents. He could honestly say being on a tight budget wasn't the worst thing in the world, not when you had someone to share life's ups and downs with.

Tess seemed to be carrying a lot of those downs by herself. He didn't want her to be worried about her dad, the ranch and bills with Christmas right around the corner. If he offered to help, it would leave him vulnerable. But if he didn't, could he live with himself?

"I tell you what," Sawyer said. "I'll take a temporary pay cut. Half my salary—" he raised his hands, palms out, near his chest "—on the condition I'm able to make the changes needed to bring in more income and reduce expenses."

Only a few feet separated them, and she tilted her chin up. Gratitude and confusion swirled in her expression. "You would do that?"

"Temporarily." He nodded, although his head started screaming not to do it.

Too late now. Once more, he was voluntarily making sacrifices for a woman, and she was the one who had everything to gain while he had everything to lose.

"I can't let you." She shook her head. "It wouldn't be fair."

He should have been relieved. She seemed to shrivel inside herself, though.

"If it were up to me," she said, "I'd give you free rein, but it isn't. I don't have the authority to let you make changes."

Her honesty touched him. He had eighteen years of experience dealing with a tough rancher—his father. "Leave your dad to me. I'll get him to see things my way."

He'd regret this at some point, but for now it felt right.

"If you can get Daddy to see anything other than his way, I'd be shocked."

"You got him to accept treatment for his cancer, didn't you?" He assumed Ken would have balked at the idea of chemo or radiation—anything that would take him away from the cattle and remind him of his mortality.

"Ye-e-s." A smile teased her lips. "He wasn't exactly receptive to it until I convinced him."

"See? He can be reasonable. Don't worry."

"You clearly don't know me." She let out a soft sigh. "Worry is my middle name."

He wanted to take those worries and make them disappear.

Too dangerous. When it came to work, he trusted his instincts. But women? He was a softhearted fool when it came to a damsel in distress.

After Christina's deception, he'd thought his life was over. But God had helped him patch together some self-respect and a purpose. He couldn't throw away either now, not when he'd been given a second chance to have the life he wanted.

"If you can cut expenses and figure out how to bring in more income, the pay cut wouldn't last long." Tess stared at him with a thoughtful expression. "You'd basically be finding the money to pay yourself."

Trust issues or not, his father would want him to get the ranch back on track. He met her gaze head-on. "Does this mean we have an agreement?"

She shouldn't be letting him make this sacrifice, but what choice did she have? The divorce settlement had left her with next to nothing since their sole asset had been a heavily mortgaged house. She and Devin had gotten an estimate on the equity in it, and he'd paid her cash for her half, barely covering her lawyer's bills. Currently, her only income was Devin's child support payments.

Tess could feel a headache coming on. Maybe it was time to get a job. But who would take care of Tucker? And what about her dad? She wanted to shut her eyes and pretend this wasn't happening. While she appreciated Sawyer's offer, it seemed wrong for him to be the one sacrificing for their ranch.

If there was anything else she could do...

"This place can be profitable, Tess." He'd taken a step toward her. He looked so sincere—so lean and strong and calm. "I know what needs to be done."

A whisper in her head taunted—could she really trust him?

She shushed it. The man standing before her had devoted hours upon hours of work to fix up the property. The only reason not to trust him at this point was his past, and it wasn't like hers was paved in perfection.

"I think you're underestimating how stubborn Daddy can be. Whatever changes you want to make will be met with resistance."

"I'm sure you're right. We'll do what we can." He placed his hand on her shoulder, and her nerve endings fizzled. What she wouldn't do to be able to lean into him, let him take charge. "Just try to enjoy the Christmas season. You have a lot to deal with. Leave the ranch to me."

She did have a lot to deal with.

But she couldn't leave it all to him. Wouldn't. Not after Devin.

"Thank you for doing this," she said. "But so we're clear, I'm not going to just leave the ranch to you. I'll still be out there every day, and I expect to be kept in the loop."

Appreciation flashed in his eyes. He took his hand off her shoulder, and she immediately missed the contact. "You have my word."

"Good."

The air between them felt like the eerie calm before a storm.

"I guess we have a deal, then," he said.

"I guess we do."

Sawyer didn't seem the type to pat her on the head and do his own thing. But she owed it to her father to make sure he had the ranch's best interests in mind. She owed it to herself, too. More than the ranch was on the line. She'd let her voice be silenced in the past, and she would never let it happen again. Especially not when this cowboy tempted her to leave it all in his capable hands. She couldn't afford to. She had too much to lose.

Chapter Four

December arrived with snow, making the chores more of a challenge. Sawyer tucked his chin against the wind as he walked back to the pole barn after taking care of Pansy. Each day he rotated between the horses to give them exercise, and Pansy was his favorite. It had been a long, bitterly cold day of checking cattle and doing emergency repairs. All weekend, he'd been brainstorming the best short-term decisions to make long-term profits for the ranch.

He fully expected Ken to resist change, but could the man be persuaded to try some of Sawyer's suggestions?

Earlier, Tess had come out to the stables and invited Sawyer to eat supper with them. Apparently, her father had finished a round of chemo a few days ago and was feeling up for a visitor. Sawyer both dreaded and looked forward to the meal. He dreaded running his ideas past Ken, but he looked forward to sharing a meal with Tess.

The more he got to know her, the more he liked her. Every day when she stopped by, he learned a little bit more about her. She lived on coffee, had a great head for numbers, was frugal and adored her son. He liked the kid, too.

Whenever Tuck ran up to him with his arms in the air, yelling, "Soy, twac, twac!" Sawyer couldn't help but grin. The toddler's limited vocabulary, the way he pointed to the tractor and bounced until Sawyer sat him on his lap up there... Well, it made his heart light.

After making sure the UTV and equipment had been returned properly, Sawyer covered the bin of trucks and Tonka tractors he'd found in the storage room and nudged it next to the wall. He'd cleared a space for Tuck to play with them while he and Tess talked.

Maybe he could add a few decorations out here. Fashion wreaths from the juniper and cedar trees on the property. He had extra bows in his cabin. It would make the season a little brighter for everyone. He didn't have time tonight, though.

He locked up the pole barn and strode to his cabin. Every time he saw the small building, a surge of warmth filled him.

Home.

He was home.

Inside, he took off his coat and boots and went straight to the shower. Ten minutes later, when he'd cleaned up and dressed, a text came through from Austin.

Tomorrow night. Mac's place after the Advent service. We will drag you there if you don't show.

Sawyer chuckled, then grimaced. He had no doubt they'd do it, too.

With jittery hands, he texted back. Okay. I'll be there. Shoving the phone in his pocket, he went back to the bathroom to make sure he was presentable. His button-down shirt and jeans were neither too dressy nor too casual. Just right.

Did it really matter what he was wearing? It wasn't like this was a date.

He kind of wished it were a date.

Making a point to wear his clean cowboy boots and his good coat, he reached for the front door handle. Christmas tree lights twinkled at him. Taking a quick look around, a surge of Christmas spirit lifted his spirits. Trimmed evergreen branches covered the mantel. A basket of pine cones he'd collected sat on the table. And throughout the room he'd tucked bunches of small red berries he'd gathered.

It was a welcome haven after long, cold days on the ranch.

Outside once more, he navigated his way down the path to the farmhouse, mentally reviewing what he wanted to discuss with Ken. Did he mention his pasture idea or did he get wild and suggest combining two of the small herds?

He didn't know. He just didn't know. *God, will You lead me tonight?*

Moments later, Tess ushered him inside. Her cheeks were flushed, lips dark red, and she wore a long red sweater over black leggings.

Tucker ran up, grinning. "Soy!"

"Hey, Tuck." Sawyer laughed as the boy plowed into his arms. He picked him up and settled him on his hip. "Were you good for your mama today?"

"Me help." He jabbed his thumb into his little chest. His light brown hair, sparkling brown eyes, chubby cheeks and sturdy body all added up to adorable. Ladybug patiently thumped her tail for Sawyer to pet her, and he was happy to oblige.

He glanced at Tess, who watched them with a thoughtful expression. "Tuck put the napkins on the table for me."

"That's good of you to help your mama." Sawyer set him back on his feet. He ran away, his socks slipping on the hardwood.

"Be careful!" Tess called after him, then shook her head, exasperated. "He has two speeds. Zero and ten. Nothing in between."

"Having a lot of energy isn't a bad thing." He took off his boots and coat and followed her to the dining room, where Ken sat at the head of the table and Tucker was climbing up onto a chair with a booster seat strapped to it. Sawyer sprang into action, easily lifting the boy into the seat. "Here, let me help."

"Thanks." Tess smiled, meeting his eyes, as she rounded the chair to buckle Tucker in.

"Don't mention it." He trapped her gaze a beat longer than he should have, then forced himself to sit on the other side of the table. He nodded to Ken. "Good to see you again, sir."

"Call me Ken." The man looked much better than the last time Sawyer had been here. He wasn't as pale and his eyes held a gleam as he watched Tucker reach for the toddler silverware Tess had set for him.

"We eat, Papa!" Tucker clutched the spoon in one hand.

"Yes, we do. Let's see what fine meal your mom made for us today."

"Whatever it is, it smells terrific." Sawyer caught Tess's glance as she set a steaming platter on the table. She blushed.

"Chicken Parmesan. Hope everyone's hungry." She took her seat. "Daddy, would you lead the prayer?"

Ken said a table prayer, and soon they were all wrapping noodles around their forks and biting into the ooey-gooey mozzarella-covered breaded chicken. If Sawyer could have only one meal the rest of his life, this would be it.

"This is delicious. Thank you, Tess. I didn't know you were such a good cook." Sawyer met her eyes across the table.

"Thanks. I like cooking. I learned a lot from the chefs at my ex's restaurants."

Her ex. He angled his neck, watching her, wondering what had happened. Had she loved the guy? He couldn't imagine anyone being dumb enough to let her go.

"Sawyer, update me on the cattle." Ken reached for a slice of garlic bread. "Any rougher for the wear since the snow hit?"

Shaking away thoughts of Tess and her ex-husband, Sawyer shifted his attention to Ken. "They all survived. Some of the old fencing didn't, though."

Now was as good a time as any to get the man used to Sawyer's idea of combining two of the herds into one.

"You and Bud fixing it?" Ken asked.

Bud. There was another problem he'd have to address at some point. Not tonight, though.

"Actually, I wanted to run something else by you."

The man's eyebrows drew together as he scowled. "Well, go on."

"The fencing between the northeast pasture and the north pasture has several breaks. I think we should combine both herds and let them spread out between them."

"Nonsense." Ken stabbed a forkful of chicken and

took his time chewing. "The smaller herds forage better by themselves. And it would be a waste of fencing. One big pasture?" He shook his head as if it were the stupidest thing he'd ever heard.

Tess's eyes widened, but she diverted her attention to her pasta. Sawyer wasn't put off by Ken's words. "I know it seems that way, but it's easy to check one larger herd. Takes more time to switch pastures and check two. Plus, I can salvage the fencing separating the pastures to repair the other ones."

"I always keep small herds. Better pasture management."

"I understand." Sawyer sipped his water, undeterred by Ken's reluctance. He knew exactly how to play this. "Where do you buy your barbed wire? We'll need a lot of it. Do you have an account with a local store? I'll keep feeding the herds separately, and Bud and I will continue to rake up the excess hay as best we can in both pastures."

Tucker let out a squeal. His face was orange with spaghetti sauce, and he had bits of noodles on his chin. He was valiantly trying to get a grip on a strand of pasta. Tess sighed as she scraped the boy's noodles into a pile for him to easily eat. Her smile, brimming with maternal affection, made Sawyer momentarily forget where he was and why he was there.

What would it be like to be filled with the love and pride of being a parent?

"Waste, huh?" Ken finally responded. "How much are we talking?"

Sawyer shook the thoughts free and began outlining the overlap of costs in keeping both pastures open. Ken asked questions. Sawyer did his best to answer them. They all finished eating, and Tess attempted to wash

Tucker's hands and face with a warm washcloth as the boy hollered. Then Ken pushed back from the table and said the words Sawyer wanted to hear.

"All right. Combine the two herds. Just those two, mind you. Leave the others alone. Wait to take down that fence. I want to be sure what you're proposing actually works."

"There's a long section of it damaged. I'll remove the wire from that part. I can take care of the rest in the spring."

"How are you going to bring the herds together?" Ken leaned back in his chair, seeming to warm to the topic.

Sawyer gave him a grin. "How else? With food."

They both chuckled and talked more until Ken set his napkin next to the plate and excused himself. "I'm going to my room. Thank you, Tess, for the meal."

"You're welcome, Daddy." She unstrapped Tucker, all cleaned up, and lifted him out of the seat. As soon as his feet hit the floor, he raced to Ken and wrapped his chubby arms around Ken's legs, looking up at him with a toothy grin.

"Night, Papa!"

"Night, squirt."

Sawyer stood and helped clear the table. As he and Tess reached for an empty plate, her hand brushed his. He let her take it. Being near her affected his equilibrium. Did he affect her, too?

Once they'd finished clearing everything, Sawyer couldn't think of a reason to stay. But he wanted to. The house had been decorated with colorful lights and old-fashioned ornaments. Homey. Nice.

"Well, I'll be heading back," he said. "Thanks, again,

for the meal. It was the best thing I've eaten in a long time."

Tess's mouth opened as if she wanted to say something, but she didn't.

"See you tomorrow." He made his way to the front hall. She followed him, leaning her shoulder against the wall as he prepared to leave.

"You handled him well."

He knew she referred to Ken. "Yeah, well, I have some experience with ranchers."

"Thank you." Her eyes shone, and he had a feeling she was thanking him for more than just how he'd handled her father, but for the life of him, he had no idea what.

"You're welcome." He nodded, opened the door and stepped outside. Another minute with her and he would have done something stupid. Like invite himself to stay longer.

The cold air on the walk home would do him a world of good. He had no business dreaming of anything more than friendship with the boss's daughter.

Ah, this was what she'd been longing for—a few hours with no men. Just an afternoon of baking Christmas cookies with her friend Hannah Carr and Hannah's mom, Patty. Hannah's sister-in-law Leann was upstairs in the toy room keeping Tucker and her own two-year-old son, Cam, occupied.

Tess and Hannah had been good friends in high school, and Tess relied on her and the Mayer sisters, Erica and Reagan, for much-needed female input since moving back to Sunrise Bend. Whenever being surrounded by cattle-obsessed ranchers got old, Tess came to Carr Ranch for some girl time.

"And I told Shelly to mind her own business, but did she?" Patty—plump, generous and active in church—in addition to her love of baking, got things done and excelled at chitchat. She wore a red sweater topped with a forest green apron. Her big glasses showcased sparkling eyes. "We didn't even have a chance to take a vote. No one wants veggie burgers for the Advent supper. No one. Ever. Can you imagine me trying to get Frank to eat a burger not made of meat?"

Tess laughed. She could not imagine Patty's husband, Frank, eating one. Patty and Frank were about the same age as her dad was and her mom would have been had Mom lived. Pneumonia had taken her when Tess was a small child. Times like this, she missed having a mom.

Sometimes she missed her ex in-laws, too. Until the divorce, Tess had enjoyed spending time with them. Sure, they could be overbearing and their son could do no wrong in their eyes, but it had been nice to drop in to see them on weekends and spend the holidays together. No doubt, they were spending their time with Devin's new family now. The grip of envy squeezed her lungs.

Patty bustled near the stove. "It's like Shelly is single-handedly trying to ruin Advent suppers. Well, I insisted tonight is chili and corn bread. Dixie and I already have it warming in the Crock-Pots at church." The timer went off, and Patty pressed the button, then bent to check on the cookies in the oven. "Almost there. I'll give them another minute."

Hannah had lined up bowls of colored frosting and bottles of sprinkles on the counter. She taught third grade at the elementary school and had taken a vacation day to bake. Tess was so glad she had. Hannah addressed

Patty. "Remind me to leave a dozen for Sunni to decorate after school."

Sunni was Leann's five-year-old daughter. Tess never tired of hearing about Leann and Michael's swoony love story. On her way into town a few years ago, Leann's car had slid off the road during a snowstorm, and Hannah's brother Michael rescued her and Sunni.

Tess's romance with Devin had not been as dramatic, and it certainly hadn't resulted in a lifelong love. Still, hearing their tale gave her a glimmer of hope that true love did exist.

"I will, and speaking of extra cookies…" Patty's voice lilted at the end. Hannah glanced at Tess and mouthed, *Here we go.* "I'm making some of those Peanut Blossoms Randy and Austin like so much. Be sure to drop them off on your way home."

"I'm not driving all the way out to their ranch, Mom."

"I know that. I'm talking about Randy's store. Don't fight me, either. You drive past it every day." Patty shook her head as if Hannah didn't have a clue. Then she turned her attention to Tess. "How's Sawyer settling in? I always liked him. He was younger than Michael and David, but he sure was respectful whenever I ran into him in town or at church. I hope to see him out and about soon."

"He's settling in fine." Tess grew uncomfortably warm. She didn't want to talk about Sawyer. Probably because she didn't know how she felt about him. As much as she wanted to put him in the same box as Devin and her dad—dismissive and overbearing—she couldn't. Sawyer put a lot of thought into his actions and wasn't afraid to ask for advice.

She was really starting to like the guy.

After supper last night, she'd wanted him to stay. She'd

almost asked him to, but thankfully her good sense had silenced her.

"Grew up to be handsome, too, from what I hear." Patty opened the oven and took out two sheets of cut-out cookies. "Haven't seen him around myself, but Janet caught a glimpse of him pumping gas last week."

Yes, he was handsome. Too handsome. Tess squeezed drops of red food coloring into a bowl of frosting, hoping her cheeks didn't match. "I guess. If you like the tall, lean, muscly type."

"Can't go wrong with that combination." Hannah shrugged, an innocent look on her face. "What's he like? I barely remember him."

"He's a hard worker. Laid-back. He has a surfer vibe, but he's all cowboy. It's hard to describe." Tess directed her attention to the sprinkles shaped like bells and stars. She'd said too much. Surfer vibe? All cowboy?

"A surfer cowboy." Patty held up the spatula as she beamed. "Sounds perfect for one of you girls."

Hannah grinned. "I might have to drive out to your place and get a lookie-loo for myself."

Hannah's blond hair, blue eyes, long legs and slender frame added up to all-American beauty. She had a joyful personality and was generous, so generous. Tess sighed. How Hannah was still single was beyond her. Sawyer would fall head over heels for her in a hot minute. What guy wouldn't?

Jealousy crept into her heart. She didn't want Sawyer and Hannah becoming a thing. *Yeah, and why is that? You want him for yourself, don't you? Have you forgotten how your last relationship went?*

"It's been good for Daddy having Sawyer in charge

of things. He's actually been staying indoors, where he belongs."

"How is he doing, hon?" Patty deftly moved the cookies from the trays onto the cooling racks.

"Better. This last round of chemo really wiped him out, though." Her throat tightened as she thought of the past month. She'd watched him get sicker and sicker until she'd grown sure he'd die soon. Then he'd slowly rebounded. Yesterday had been the best she'd seen him in a long time, but he still needed to take it easy. "I'm already anticipating a struggle with him. He'll want to ride out with Sawyer soon, but he's supposed to be resting."

"Your dad is stubborn, for sure." Patty pointed the spatula at her. "Enlist Sawyer to help. He can motivate Ken to stay inside."

"Uh, have you met my father?" Tess tilted her head and gave her a deadpan stare.

She chuckled. "If he sees Sawyer doing a good job, he won't be so anxious to get out there and help. Sawyer is doing a good job, isn't he?"

Hannah watched her expectantly. Tess had no problem answering. "Yes, he is. He's done a lot in a short time. He's been cleaning up the place, too."

"Good. That's what I like to hear." Patty looked around the counters as if she'd lost something. "Oh, no! I'll be right back." And she hustled out of the kitchen toward the mudroom, where a large pantry was located.

Hannah shook her head in annoyance. "Can you get over her? Ordering me to drop off cookies to Randy and Austin?"

"Is she still trying to get you together with one of the Watkins boys?" Tess waggled her eyebrows.

"Ugh. Yes. I'm not interested. Why can't she get it through her head?"

"They're both easy on the eyes." Tess swiped a snicker-doodle. She bit into it and practically melted into a puddle right there on her stool. "Oh, wow. These are amazing. How does she get them so light and crisp?"

"You know Mom. She's got the touch. I can eat half a dozen of these bad boys in a sitting." Hannah scooped white frosting into a pastry bag. "I just ignore her match-making at this point. She's determined I find a *nice cowboy* from these parts. Doesn't matter if it's Austin or Randy or Jet or Blaine or Mac or the Bloom boys, who are too young for me, as you and I both know. They're all interchangeable in her mind."

"You're not interested in any of them?" Tess brushed her hands free of crumbs. She had eyes. Every man Hannah mentioned was single and gorgeous. Any one of those ranchers would make a fine husband…for Hannah. She, personally, had no desire to date or marry any of them. Or anyone, for that matter.

"You, too?" Hannah rolled her eyes and shook her head. "I thought I could escape the constant reminder of my singleness for a few hours baking Christmas cookies, but clearly I was wrong."

"Okay, I'm sorry. It's just…ever since Shawn…"

Hannah's bright smile dimmed. "Yeah."

"I get it." Tess did. "I'm not one to talk. Not after Devin…"

Neither spoke as they stared at each other for a few beats, and understanding weaved between them. Tess tilted her chin up. "We don't need men."

"Agreed." Hannah nodded smartly.

"The whole relationship thing is overrated."

"Absolutely."

The thump of footsteps from the living room made them turn.

"What did I miss?" Leann walked in, holding her phone. She propped it on the counter, where an image of Cam and Tucker sleeping side by side appeared. "They both fell asleep watching a cartoon. We can keep an eye on them here."

"Oh, good." Tess patted the stool next to her.

"You didn't miss much." Hannah grinned. "We rehashed the Advent supper drama—"

"You could have warned me last week." Leann groaned as she sat on the stool. "Michael took one look at the veggie burgers, and I'm not lying, the man paled. His face completely drained of blood." Leann widened her eyes in emphasis. "I feared he might pass out, and this from the man who has hunted his entire life. He'd been counting on baked potato soup and pulled pork sandwiches. Why did they change it?"

Patty returned, holding a bag of M&M's and chocolate chips. "I forgot the cinnamon candies."

"You always forget them." Hannah made room on the counter for the goodies. "I can bring some over tomorrow. Or do you want me to text Dad? He'll run to the store if you want."

"Hold on." Leann got up and rummaged through her diaper bag. Triumphantly, she pulled out a bag of cinnamon imperial candies. "Ta-da. I figured you'd need these."

"What would we do without you?" Patty wiped her hands off on her apron and went over to Leann, pulling her in for a hug. "I thank God every day Michael married you."

Leann hugged her back. "I thank God every day, too."

At the tender display, Tess's heart hiccuped. She'd come to the Carr ranch for girl time. But girl time wasn't the only thing missing in her life. She wished she had a mom to bake with. Sisters and sisters-in-law to joke with. A counter full of cookies to share with loved ones.

Once more, she found herself missing Devin's parents. Before the divorce, Daniel and Margaret had made her feel like part of the family. And now Devin's fiancée, Tiffany, had taken her place. They were probably spoiling little Riley at this exact moment.

Tess's throat grew tight. She tried not to feel sorry for herself, but the divorce had taken more than her husband. She missed his parents more than the man himself. Once upon a time, she'd thought she'd never be able to live without him.

It turned out she'd fallen out of love as easily as she'd fallen in it.

What did that say about her?

Maybe she was just on edge about life in general. Dealing with a sick, grumpy father, a demanding two-year-old and a way too good-looking ranch manager was difficult.

The grouchy dad and energetic toddler she could handle.

The hot cowboy, on the other hand, was hijacking her thoughts more and more.

She didn't like it.

"Tess?" Hannah frowned.

"What?" She shook her head. They must have asked her something.

"Why don't you and Tucker sit with me tonight at church?" Hannah watched her expectantly.

"I'd like that." She shut off all thoughts of Sawyer and her ex. She'd enjoy the rest of the afternoon with her friends. And she'd keep doing what she'd done for years. Count her blessings and ignore the rest.

What would his friends think of him now? Sawyer parked next to a late-model white truck in Mac's circular driveway after church that night. He got out, blowing into his cupped hands, and looked up at the sky. Millions of twinkling stars stood out against the black backdrop. Beautiful. He'd never seen stars like this in the city.

As he slowly made his way up the drive, he tried to calm the anxiety rushing through his veins. It had already been a strange evening. He'd attended the Advent service, surprised to see Tess and Tucker there sitting with Hannah Carr. He'd given them a small wave and parked it in a pew on the opposite side of the church. Austin and Randy had sidled up next to him not long after.

Several people had greeted him after the service, asking him some friendly questions and a few loaded ones he'd been careful to answer. No use giving people more things to gossip about. He told the truth but held the personal stuff close to his chest.

Afterward in the parking lot, Austin and Randy had joked around that they'd tie a chain to his truck and tow him to Mac's if he didn't follow them. So he did.

And now here he was. About to spend a few hours with the friends he'd grown up with. The ones he'd played football with in high school, the ones he'd spent all his free time with as a teen. The ones who'd known him inside and out when his dad was alive.

The ones who didn't know him now that his dad was dead.

He climbed the porch steps of the massive house decorated with white lights, a big wreath and red-and-green-plaid bows. He stood on the doorstep in between two wire reindeer lit with white Christmas lights for a few moments and tried to get himself together. Shame swirled through him. All these years later and he still couldn't escape the embarrassment of his bad choices.

Would they judge him for it?

The door opened to Mac's broad smile. He was about the same height as Sawyer but beefier, all muscle. Sawyer had always thought Mac would make a good hockey player.

"Get in here, man." Mac pulled him inside and embraced him, clapping him on the back twice before stepping back. "You're finally here. We've been waiting for you."

Sawyer had a feeling Mac meant more than just tonight, that they'd been waiting for him for years. Maybe that was wishful thinking, though.

He followed him into the huge great room. A floor-to-ceiling stacked stone fireplace rose up the center of the wall. Hardwood floors made the space feel inviting, and comfortable furniture was arranged on area rugs. An enormous television stood off to the side. "Nice place."

"Beats the old farmhouse Dad insisted on tearing down." Mac rolled his eyes. "Remember it?"

Sawyer nodded. "We spent some fun times in that old house."

"Yeah, well—" he raised his eyebrows to the ceiling "—nothing but the best for Dad."

"How is he?" Sawyer remembered Mac's father—a wealthy investor—coming to the ranch for a few weeks at a time and flying to his other homes the rest of the year while Mac stayed in Sunrise Bend with his trusted ranch manager, Otis.

"He's good. He and my stepmom, Candace, live with Kaylee in Texas." They made their way to the eat-in kitchen, where Sawyer recognized the other guys. "Have you ever met Kaylee? She's my half sister. A freshman in high school this year."

"I haven't met her."

"She's a great kid."

Jet and Austin were huddled over one of their phones, while Blaine nodded at something Randy said. Mac cleared his throat and they all turned.

The next five minutes were filled with welcome-back half hugs and grins. Then they retreated to the great room.

"Now that you're back," Austin said, "you're officially helping with branding and weaning our calves next year."

"Ours, too." Blaine sat in a recliner and pointed to Sawyer. "We're in the process of splitting the ranch, and I need you on my team."

"Both our teams," Jet said, shooting a glare at his brother. "We all help each other out."

This was the first Sawyer had heard about them splitting the ranch. "What's going on with your ranch?"

Jet and Blaine exchanged resigned looks. Jet cracked his knuckles. "Dad hasn't been the same since Cody died."

"It's for long-term planning."

"Your sisters, too?" Sawyer remembered Erica and Reagan, but they'd been young when he moved away.

"No," Blaine said. "Erica's getting married this summer, and Reagan prefers working with Mom's candle venture. Which leaves us to divvy up the ranch. You should come out sometime. Mom and Dad would enjoy seeing you."

Emotions shot through Sawyer—gratitude, humility, sadness. If he'd known they would welcome him back with open arms, would he have stayed away so long?

"You got it." Sawyer nodded to Blaine.

"Forget all the ranching stuff," Randy said with a twinkle in his eye. "What you need is a nice long day of fishing with me. We need to catch us some bass."

Sawyer had spent more than one Saturday morning fishing with Randy back in the day. Good memories.

"What's it like working for Ken? Is it strange being on the ranch you called home most of your life?" Jet grabbed a handful of cheese popcorn from the enormous plastic bowl Mac had set on the coffee table.

"It's different." He didn't know what to say. Didn't know where to start.

"Ken's a tough rancher." Austin sat on the couch.

"He is. Reminds me of my dad in some ways." The only difference was Sawyer's dad had treated him like an heir whereas Ken viewed him as an employee. It didn't bother him. He was an employee. "He's hardheaded but wants what's best for the place."

"If he gives you too hard a time, you can always work here," Mac said.

"Same goes for me." Austin nodded.

"Or you could get out of ranching and get in the bait-and-tackle business." Randy grinned. He owned a thriving store in downtown Sunrise Bend. "Watkins' Outfitters is booming."

"He's not getting out of the ranching business." Jet shook his head in disgust. Then he addressed Sawyer. "There's a place for you on our ranch, too. Say the word."

"I appreciate it." His throat grew tight as he drowned in regrets. He'd wasted all these years avoiding them, embarrassed of himself, and here they all were—rallying behind him.

Still, he couldn't work for his friends. Ever. Not because of his pride. Because he'd told himself as a broke nineteen-year-old that from that point forward, he'd rely on himself. He would never work where he wasn't needed. And none of these guys really needed another employee.

"What's New York City like?" Blaine asked.

Finally, an easy topic. Sawyer told them about the city and how he hadn't owned a vehicle in thirteen years. How he walked everywhere or took public transportation. He shared how he'd go to Central Park all year long because he missed being out in nature. He mentioned Bridget, but didn't go into too many details. They'd made each other promises they'd both keep until the day they died.

"What's your plan moving forward, Sawyer?" Austin asked after they'd caught up and thoroughly discussed their favorite NFL team's chances at making the playoffs and the state of their respective ranches.

"Work for Ken." Sawyer saw no reason not to tell them the truth. "Save up some money. Buy a couple of acres and a house outside of town."

"Get married?" Mac asked, his eyes narrowing. "Have a couple of kids?"

"Nah." He looked down at the floor, but all he could see was Tess.

"Dude," Jet said to Mac. "Why are you bringing up marriage and kids? I've had it up to here with the church ladies trying to set me up." He lifted his hand over his head.

"Sorry," Mac said sarcastically.

"Yeah, keep that stuff to yourself." Austin shook his head. "Those old biddies have been trying to set me up with their granddaughters and nieces for years. I've had it."

"I'm not getting married," Randy stated.

"Me neither." Mac actually shuddered.

"I've got no use for it." Blaine shook his head.

"Not on my hot list, either." Jet shrugged.

They all turned to stare at Sawyer.

"Don't look at me." He raised his hands in defense. "I'm not getting married."

A collective sigh of relief rippled through them.

Sawyer wasn't surprised none of them wanted to get married, but he was surprised they were so adamant about it.

He would love to have a wife and family.

But he didn't see it happening. He didn't trust himself. He wasn't smart. Didn't have the willpower to say no. He'd sacrificed too much to a woman who was more than willing to take everything he offered and then some. Which had left him empty and broke and alone.

No, marriage wasn't in his future. He'd stick with a few acres and a house. It was safer being alone.

Chapter Five

Tess turned the key in the ignition and clenched her jaw in frustration as the engine wheezed and sputtered. *Come on.* Tucker was strapped into the car seat in the back. He happily hummed and kicked his tiny boots. She'd been looking forward to their Saturday plans. She and her little man were going into town, stopping in at all her favorite stores for some Christmas shopping and getting Tucker's picture taken on Santa's lap. That was, if her car would start.

"Need some help?" Sawyer tapped on her window and she jumped. He must have heard her ancient car gasping its last breaths. She cracked open the door.

"I'm not sure there's much that will help the old gal at this point." She'd been driving the white Chevy Malibu since she'd turned sixteen. Daddy had bought it used. It had been in great shape at the time, but now? *Rusty* and *temperamental* were the best words she could come up with to describe it.

"Pop the hood. I'll take a look." His exhalation came out in spirals as he moved to the front of the car. She gladly sprang the hood's latch. Personally, she knew little about cars. If it had issues, she took it to the auto shop. Back when she'd lived in Laramie, the dealership was only a few miles away. The thirty-minute trek into Sunrise Bend made car problems a little tougher to deal with.

As Sawyer poked around under the hood, she debated what to do. She could take Daddy's truck into town, but it wouldn't solve the issue. She really needed to have the car looked at.

Sawyer straightened, returning to her door. "Might be the starter. Do you know if the battery's been replaced?"

"About two years ago." Right around the time the divorce was final. Daddy had helped her move out of their house and insisted on getting a new battery and a tune-up for the car. "If I can get it started, I'll drive straight to Fulton's Auto Repair. John's familiar with this old girl."

"Want me to give it a try?"

"Have at it." She got out and shivered as he eased his body in the driver's seat, leaving the door open. He turned the key, and the car gave it her all, but the engine failed to start.

"I have a feeling it's the alternator." Sawyer unfolded his long legs and got out of the car. "Give me a minute. I'll get my truck and the jumper cables."

She wasn't going to turn him down. "Okay." Her ex never would have jumped the car. He would have immediately called a tow truck.

Tess kind of liked having someone around who was knowledgeable about vehicle maintenance. It would certainly make it easier on her if she could drive the car to Fulton's, that was for sure.

She opened the back door and bent to check on Tucker. "Hey, buddy. How are you doing back there? You warm enough?"

He grinned. "Cocoa?"

"In a little bit." She reached over and bopped his nose with her finger. Over breakfast, she'd told him they were having a fun day with shopping and cocoa. He'd latched on to the chocolate part. Took after his mama. Her mouth watered thinking of a tower of whipped cream melting into hot chocolate. "We have to get the car running first."

"Car. Go."

"That's right." The rumble of an engine and the crunch of tires on gravel made her straighten. "Let's hope this works." She shut the back door.

Sawyer pulled his truck as close to her car as possible, then got out, slamming his door shut, and took jumper cables out of a large toolbox in the bed of his truck. In what seemed like two seconds, he had everything hooked up. He started his truck and hopped back out.

"I'm going to let it idle for a few minutes first." He'd thrown on a jacket.

"Fine by me." It sure was a relief not to have to deal with this on her own.

"If this works, I'll follow you to the auto shop. Then I can give you a ride home."

"Oh, that won't be necessary." She shivered. He'd want to drive straight back, and she didn't want to cancel her plans with Tucker. "I plan on doing some shopping. Tucker and I have a date to get hot cocoa, and then we're going to get pictures with Santa."

"How will you get home?"

She winced. She'd forgotten that part of the equation. "One of my friends could probably give me a ride." But then they'd have to drive here and back.

"I have to pick up a few things anyway. I'll follow you. You can text me when you're ready to head home."

"Oh." She was surprised. He rarely left the ranch. The only time she'd seen his truck leave was for the Advent service this week and once last weekend, which she assumed was for groceries. "Thanks. I'll take you up on it if you don't mind. We might be a while, though."

"It's okay. Take your time." His warm smile drew her attention to his mouth. And that set off a chain reaction from a rapid heartbeat to a sense of breathlessness. She couldn't look away from his face. But it wasn't his cheekbones and denim-blue eyes affecting her.

It was the fact he cared.

Sawyer was a kind man. A generous man. She didn't want to fall into the trap of thinking it had something to do with her. It didn't. It was just the kind of guy he was. He'd do this for anyone. She couldn't read more into it.

He craned his neck to the front of the car. "I'm going to try to start it."

"Do your thing." She shifted out of his way as he once more tried to fire the engine. It took a few attempts, but in the end it started.

Yes! Tess clapped her hands. Sawyer got out, brushing her arm as he stepped around her.

"Once I disconnect the cables, you can head into town. I'll be right behind you."

"Thanks." What a break. Now she wouldn't have to worry about taking Daddy's truck or having the car towed. Perfect. "I'll see you there."

As she drove down the long drive to the road leading to the highway, she cranked on a Christmas station and enjoyed the scenery. The Bighorn Mountains, bluish-purple with snowy streaks, loomed in the distance, and the white land spread out for miles. Dirty snow piles lined the road. The forecast called for more snow later, but the blue skies must not have gotten the memo yet. What a beautiful winter day.

The radio played "Deck the Halls" and Tucker did his best to keep up with the fa-la-la-la-la's, but they sounded more like lolly-lolly-la's. Coming from her little boy, she'd say it improved the song.

Half an hour later, the Welcome to Sunrise Bend sign came into view, and she drove past gas stations, a bank and a small park with a gazebo wrapped in evergreen garland and strung with lights. She took a right at the light and drove through the downtown trimmed for the holidays. The auto shop was set back on Mule Street, and in no time she'd parked the car.

Sawyer's truck pulled into the spot next to hers minutes later. She went to the back seat to get Tucker and carried him to the entrance, where Sawyer held the door open for them.

Soon she'd handed her keys to John Fulton while Sawyer took out the car seat and put it in his truck.

"Where to first?" he asked when they'd all settled in.

"The candy store." She hadn't bought fudge since the summer, and she craved it.

"Do Joy and Leonard still run it?" He navigated the truck out of the parking lot and back downtown.

"Yes. They make fresh fudge every day. It's the most amazing thing you'll ever taste. I'm getting more than one flavor."

He glanced over at her with a lopsided grin. "I might have to buy some myself."

"Oh, you should." She nodded emphatically. "You won't regret it."

They found a parking spot on a side street two blocks

away from the candy store. Tess unbuckled Tucker and lifted him out of the seat, setting him on the sidewalk.

"You have to hold my hand, buddy." Tucker had one gear—go—and those boot-clad feet hit the ground running. She lunged for the back of his snowsuit, yanking him to a halt. "What did I say?"

"But, Mama!"

"Hold my hand or no cocoa."

He clasped her hand and they headed in the direction of the store. Sawyer seemed to be taking it all in as he strolled beside her. A few people waved to them. Tess waved back. Sawyer raised his hand briefly as if he weren't quite sure what to do.

"Relax. No one's going to bite," she teased, giving him a sideways glance.

"Promise?" His skeptical grimace made her chuckle.

"You never came back here, did you?" she asked.

He shook his head.

"How long's it been?"

"Thirteen years ago. My dad's funeral."

It was on the tip of her tongue to ask why he'd stayed away, but a pin pricked her conscience. She knew why. The whole town did.

Or did they?

What had happened in New York City? What had he done with his inheritance? Where had the money gone?

"Ah, there's Watkins' Outfitters." He hitched his chin up ahead. It was near the Sassy Lasso, her favorite clothing store, not that she could afford anything in there at the moment. Leann Carr helped her sister-in-law, Kelli, run it.

"Want to go in after the candy shop?" she asked. "I

need to get Daddy another gift, and he loves Randy's place."

"You don't mind?"

"No. Like I said, I need to get a gift anyway."

"That's not what I meant." He shook his head, averting his eyes. "You don't mind walking around with me?"

The words hit her hard. In fact, she almost stopped in her tracks, but with Tucker holding her hand so nicely, she forced her feet to continue forward.

"Of course I don't mind. Why would you think I would?"

"I don't exactly have the best reputation in these parts." He met her gaze, and she was struck by the intensity in his blue eyes.

"Then it's high time we changed that."

After getting Tucker's picture with Santa, Sawyer and Tess sat at a small round table at the town's one and only coffee shop. It had the rustic decor rarely seen in the city. The theme seemed to be moose, logs and red plaid. All in all, the place was warm and loud. They made a mean cup of hot chocolate, too. Tucker had wolfed down two sugar cookies as he'd waited for his cocoa to cool, and, after making sure the lid on his child's cup was snug, Tess sipped hers slowly.

If anyone would have told Sawyer a few months ago he'd be sitting in a coffee shop with a gorgeous single mom and her cute kid in full view of the entire population of Sunrise Bend, he would have laughed in that person's face. But here he was. He supposed anything was possible.

Earlier they'd browsed Watkins' Outfitters. Sawyer had chatted with Randy while Tess picked out gifts for

Ken. A few locals had seemed taken aback to see him. One had joked about him finally getting tired of the city. And another—a guy two years older than him who used to be one of his father's ranch hands—had muttered something about how the mighty had fallen.

Sawyer hadn't bothered acknowledging him. What could he have said? It was the truth.

Then Tess had breezed to the counter with her confident smile, and the guy had straightened, offering to help her carry the fleece jacket she was purchasing. She'd flicked the guy a withering glare and curtly said she could handle it.

Sawyer tried not to stare at the brown-eyed beauty sitting across from him, but he couldn't stop thinking about her. Did she miss her ex? Why had they split? Why wasn't the guy ever around to see Tucker? What was her life like before moving back?

Like he could ask her any of those things. He couldn't. Just because she didn't mind walking around town with him didn't give him the right to probe into personal matters.

"I can't wait to dive into the cookies-and-cream fudge later." She smiled, holding her mug between her hands.

"Not the rocky road?" He'd admired her enthusiasm when she'd purchased slices of four different fudges. He'd gotten himself a piece of peanut butter fudge for later.

"No, the rocky road is for Daddy if he can stomach it. It's always been his favorite." Her wistful expression touched him.

"How long has he had cancer?"

"It's going on three years now. We found out not long after my husband—ex-husband—told me it was over." She glanced down at Tucker. Both his chubby hands encased the cardboard cup as he tipped it for another drink. "After the divorce, I moved back home to help Daddy. Tuck was a baby at the time."

Her eyes met his, and he frowned at the sadness and bravado gleaming in them.

"That was good of you." He nodded, unsure what to say.

"Oh, don't go thinking I'm selfless. I'm not. I was more than ready to leave Laramie. You've probably heard the story by now. My ex, Devin, was cheating on me with one of the managers. They are now engaged and have a daughter, Riley. She's six months younger than Tuck."

He tried not to wince. Her matter-of-fact tone hid a lot of pain. She took another drink of her cocoa.

"You kept the books, huh?" The clues were filling in some of the questions he had about her, but a lot of blank space remained.

"Yes, but unofficially. His parents own a chain of Italian restaurants. They gave Devin two of them to run while they retained ownership. The restaurants provided all our income, so I wanted them to succeed whether I was a formal employee or not. If I would have known he was going to leave me, I…"

Sawyer was tempted to reach over and tell her it was okay. He understood—maybe not everything she was feeling, but regrets? He recognized them. Lived with them daily. And he didn't want her to suffer from them, too.

"Anyway, the divorce settlement left a lot to be desired. My ex lost interest in Tucker after Tiffany delivered Riley, so the visitation arrangement was a nonissue. With Daddy being sick, it just made sense to move in with him. I'm glad I did. He's stayed pretty healthy up until recently. The ranch got to be too much for him by late summer."

Sawyer couldn't wrap his head around a guy choosing to walk away from this woman and his son. It made no sense. Didn't he have a clue how blessed he was? And to leave them vulnerable financially... He clenched his teeth together.

"Mo' cocoa, Mama." Tucker tried to pry off the plastic lid. Tess gently took the cup from him.

"One is plenty. You have so much sugar running through your veins, you could probably fly Santa's sleigh with Rudolph and the other reindeer." She kissed the top of his head and took out a sheet of stickers, a small notebook and a few crayons to keep him occupied. Then she directed her attention back to Sawyer. "What about you? Ever been married?"

"No." Heat flashed to his face. A lively Christmas tune played in the background, and the bell above the door clanged as more customers entered.

"No one special?" She cocked her head.

"Once. A long time ago." He didn't want to have this conversation. Probably should have lied and told her there'd never been anyone.

"What happened?"

"Doesn't matter."

It did matter. Mattered more than he cared to admit. He'd made a mistake. A monumental mistake. And though he hadn't missed Christina in many years, he missed the feeling he'd had when they'd started dating. The way she'd looked at him like he was something special. The unbelievable heady intoxication of being one half of a couple, of feeling invincible with her by his side. He'd thought he'd have forever with her.

He'd fallen in love with her so hard it had knocked the sense right out of him.

When she'd told him if he loved her, he'd add her name to his bank account, he'd done it the next day. She was determined, and he'd liked that about her. Christina told everyone and anyone she was going to be the next pop sensation. If willpower alone could have gotten her there, Sawyer figured she'd be famous by now.

He'd funded every demo, every costume, every limo ride, every plane ticket to meet someone who might influence her career. The expensive apartment, the band fees. And he'd funded other things, too. Things he hadn't known about. Things he'd found out when his bank account was empty and his apartment was, too.

"Was it Bridget?" The too-blasé note in Tess's tone had him looking up at her. If he didn't know better, he'd think it hinted at jealousy. *Don't be stupid. Like Tess would ever be jealous over you.*

"No." He drank the last of his coffee, setting the cup down. "She's like my little sister. Neither of us have ever thought of each other like that."

"You said she's still in New York, right?"

"Yeah. Believe it or not, she's manager of a coffee shop—a fancy one, though."

"No moose heads or log walls?" Her lips twitched in amusement.

"No. Black walls, those old-timey bare light bulbs dangling from the ceiling. Tables with matchsticks for legs, a long stainless-steel counter and names of drinks I can't pronounce." His heart grew lighter thinking about it. "She'd like this place, though."

"Sunrise Bend?"

"Yeah, and this coffee shop."

"Is that where you met her?" Tess hauled Tucker on her lap as he rubbed his eyes and sank back against her chest with a big yawn.

"We worked together at a diner." He didn't mind opening up more about his past, as long as it didn't involve Christina.

"So we both were in the food industry." She wrapped her arms around the boy and rested her chin on the top of his head.

"Yes." But he'd been a lowly employee, not in charge of the books or married to the owner. "It wasn't my first choice. I always loved ranching. After my mom died, I grew real close to my dad. Helped him with the ranch every day. I miss him."

"What happened to your mom?"

"She died when I was ten. Burst appendix. Yours?"

"Pneumonia took her when I was four." She relaxed as Tucker's eyelids drooped. "I don't remember much about her. Daddy told me all about how she loved Christmas. I'm having a hard time wrapping my head around the fact I might be spending Christmases without both parents in the near future."

"I'm not going to sugarcoat it, Tess. It's hard." His gaze locked with hers. "I'd do about anything to have one more Christmas morning checking cattle with my dad. Sharing a thermos of coffee and a big batch of sticky buns from the bakery in town. Opening presents and sitting around the tree for hours just hanging out. I miss that. I miss him."

"You really love the ranch, don't you?"

"Yeah, I do."

"I know what you mean." Tucker had fallen asleep. "I always try to make Christmas festive for Daddy the way my mother did, and he appreciates it. He spoiled me silly on Christmas. When I was in high school, he'd buy stacks of clothes for me—I had to return most of them for a different size, but his heart was in the right place. And even now, we love exchanging a pile of gifts, doesn't matter if they're store-bought or homemade. Christmas brings out Daddy's happy side."

Sawyer could picture Ken doting on Tess. He'd made it clear time and again she was the apple of his eye. Sawyer could see why. Smart, generous, strong—she checked all his own boxes.

"Did you go to school for bookkeeping?" he asked.

"Not really." One shoulder lifted in a shrug. "I have a business degree. I taught myself the financial side."

"A business degree." He whistled. Another reason to add to his growing list of why Tess was off-limits. She was way out of his league. He'd graduated from high school with mediocre grades, and he'd never even considered college. "I wouldn't be surprised if some of the businesses around here could use someone like you taking care of their books."

Her eyes grew round. "You have a point. I could take care of their billing, send invoices, reconcile their books. I did that and more for the restaurants, not that my ex would listen to me." She let out a little laugh at the end, but Sawyer frowned.

"Why wouldn't he listen to you?"

"That's the million-dollar question, Sawyer." Her eyes darkened, and the corner of her mouth lifted in a sad smile. "Why don't the men in my life ever listen to me?"

The following afternoon while Tucker napped, Tess sat at the kitchen counter with her laptop, a notebook, pen and mug of hot tea. A gentle snow fell outside, and instrumental Christmas music played softly through a Bluetooth speaker nearby. Ever since Sawyer had mentioned offering her bookkeeping services to businesses in Sunrise Bend, her brain had been on fire with ideas of how to make it happen. Now she finally had the time to dig into researching what she needed to do.

Yesterday had been unexpected. Instead of a special day with her and her boy, it had turned into an even better day with Sawyer joining them. She'd been surprised when he went into every store with her. His comment about his reputation had sliced down her heart. Until that moment, she hadn't realized how embarrassed he was to be back in town.

He had no reason to be embarrassed.

Sure, only a few weeks ago she'd thought he was a loser, but that was just because she hadn't known him. And checking in with him all these afternoons, seeing the improvements he made, watching him work night and day to make the ranch succeed—well, she was proud to stroll the sidewalks of Sunrise Bend with him by her side.

He'd taken her and Tucker to church this morning since her car was still in the shop. They'd sat together, and she'd fought to keep her focus on the pastor when it kept zooming to Sawyer sitting inches away. Tucker had climbed onto his lap during the sermon, and he'd smiled down at her son with such tenderness she'd blinked away sudden tears.

The only person besides her who looked at Tucker with that much affection was her father.

She sipped her coffee. Tucker should have a daddy, too. Was Devin playing with Riley right now, making Christmas memories with her and Tiffany? They'd announced their engagement the day after Tess and Devin's divorce was final. What a slap in the face.

She sighed. Back then, Devin had assured her he wanted to be part of Tucker's life. He'd agreed to joint custody. She'd been relieved. The last thing she wanted for Tuck was to be estranged from his father.

But, like everything else Devin committed to, he'd broken his promise.

For three months, Devin had taken Tucker every other weekend. Those weekends without her baby had about killed her, but she'd accepted them as his right. And it wasn't as if he'd taken care of Tucker on his own. She'd found out he basically drove the baby straight to his parents for them to babysit.

Then Tiffany had delivered a bouncing baby girl, and neither Devin nor his parents had wanted the weekends with Tucker anymore. Little Riley had squeezed out Tess's son.

She inhaled sharply. Why was she thinking about this now? She had bigger things to deal with—exciting things—not bitter memories involving her ex. She'd put those days behind her. Accepted them. Moved on.

But those moments yesterday with Sawyer had reminded her of her broken dreams of a family.

He'd proudly carried Tucker through the Sassy Lasso while Tess tried on a clearance sweater. Then he'd made funny faces when Tuck's lips wobbled as he tried to decide if Santa was a friend or foe. Sawyer didn't seem to think the boy was a third wheel but a vital member of the team.

Will you stop glamorizing him? Just because he's patient and humble and hardworking and cute... Who said he was cute? Oh, right, you did.

Tess rubbed the back of her neck. She was wasting precious nap time. Opening a web browser on her laptop, she started typing in the research items on her list. Since she wanted to make her own schedule, she figured offering her services as a freelancer would be the best option.

She spent the next hour taking notes, researching more details as they came up and getting a better idea of what she needed to do. Shuffling noises from the hall alerted her Daddy was on the move. He came into view moments later.

Studying him as she did every day, she noted his color was good and he'd taken the time to shower and put on fresh sweatpants and a sweatshirt. All positive signs.

"Got a cup of coffee for me, Tessie-girl?" He sat on the stool next to her. He tried to hide it, but she could tell he was winded.

"Coming right up." She stood and kissed his cheek. Then she turned to the kitchen, arching her back to stretch it out. "Want cream and sugar?"

"You know I take it black." His eyes twinkled.

"And you know I like to make afternoon coffee a treat."

"Okay, I'll try it your way." He didn't sound upset. He secretly loved the flavored creamer she added. "Are you putting some of that fancy whipped cream on top?"

Opening the fridge, she suppressed a smile. He'd never admit it, but he liked spray-can whipped cream, too, and who could blame him? "I am."

"If I have to drink it that way…"

She poured a healthy dose of caramel-flavored creamer into a mug, filled it with coffee and sprayed a small mountain of whipped cream on top before bringing it over to him. "Here you go."

"Ah…" He took a sip, the whipped cream dotting his nose. They both laughed. Then he wiped it off. "Whatcha workin' on there?"

"I'm thinking about offering my bookkeeping services to local businesses."

"What would you do that for?" He turned to face her, his forehead wrinkling.

"I do have a son to support." She almost added a *duh*, but Daddy wouldn't appreciate it.

"Don't you go worrying about money." His cheeks flushed. "I'm taking care of you."

"I'm a grown woman. I can provide for myself."

"But winter's here. I don't want you driving all over the county, getting blown off the road, doing someone's job they should be doing themselves."

"I'll be able to do most of the work from home, so don't worry about me blowing off the road."

"Well, what about Tuck? Who's going to watch him while you're fiddling around?"

"*I* will, Daddy." *Fiddling around?* She sighed, closing the laptop, no longer enthused about research. "I plan on doing this part-time. I can work while he naps or after he goes to bed."

"What if you get more business than you can handle?"

"I'll be my own boss. I can say no." She was this close to saying no to listening to any more of his objections. "Tucker's getting older. I can have him doing activities with me at the table while I get things done."

"Bah!" He shook his head as if she'd suggested buying a spaceship and flying away to another galaxy. "He'll run off and get into trouble, and you'll get mad and won't get nothin' done."

"Gee, thanks for your support."

"Like I said, I'll take care of you and Tuck. Don't worry about it."

She opened her mouth to argue, but it wasn't worth it. He didn't understand that she liked to work. And even if she didn't, their finances weren't in good shape. Sawyer had taken a pay cut and was working long hours. How could she look him in the eye and not pursue this when she could easily take on a few clients to bring in extra money?

She couldn't.

And it did no good trying to convince her father. Since she didn't know how much time she had left with him, she'd make every minute count.

"What do you say we watch a Christmas movie?" She hitched her thumb toward the living room. "Your choice. What was the one Mom loved so much?"

"Home Alone."

"I'll put it in. Take your coffee with you. Want me to fix us a plate of cookies, too?"

"I don't turn down cookies."

"Neither do I." She kept her tone breezy, but inside her frustration hung on. Why couldn't her father trust her for once? Why did he have to question every decision she made?

He was always telling her he'd take care of her and Tucker, but for all his talk, she had a hard time taking him seriously.

The reality was that she'd been taking care of Daddy for years. She couldn't rely on a man to take care of her. She had to take care of herself.

Chapter Six

Was this a way to bring in a large sum of money for the ranch? Sawyer inspected the old tractor in one of the outbuildings he'd finally taken the time to explore. It didn't look like it was in working condition, but he was pretty sure it could be fixed. And the fact Ken owned a late-model tractor meant this one could be sold. Sawyer patted one of its dusty tires before exiting the shed. His eyes took a minute to adjust to the afternoon brightness.

Another Monday in the great outdoors. No place he'd rather be.

The weekend had been unexpected. Never in his best dreams had he expected to slide back into Sunrise Bend with such ease. In New York City, he'd been convinced his hometown would condemn him, look down on him. For the most part, though, people had welcomed him back like he hadn't been the worst kind of fool.

Austin and the guys had paved the way, sure, but strolling around town with Tess and Tucker had sealed the deal. It was clear she was respected in these parts, and if Sawyer was good enough for her to be seen with, well, he must not be too much of a screwup in their minds. At least, that was what he assumed was going on. How else could he explain the waves and howdies he'd received Saturday and yesterday at church?

Sawyer shivered beneath his coat and marched along the frozen dirt toward the pole barn. The snow had melted yesterday, but an overnight freeze had packed the earth solid. He still intended to lie low. Work hard and give no one anything to gossip about. He'd given them enough after Dad died.

Soon Tess would bring Tucker out to the pole barn. Had she thought more about the bookkeeping service? He hadn't seen her after church yesterday. He usually didn't on Sundays, though. Hopefully Ken was still doing okay. Some days he sounded better than others. Sawyer would have to figure out the best way to bring up the topic of selling the old tractor. There were a few other machines they could sell, too.

Opening the pole barn door, he took a moment to mentally assess the space. The floors no longer had mud caked on them. All of the boxes and parts strewn about when he'd first arrived had been packed and moved to a storage room he'd cleared out. The tractor he used daily had plenty of empty space on either side.

Where was the UTV?

Bud had checked on the newly combined herd with him this morning. He'd told Sawyer he would feed the steers before taking off for the day. Frankly, Sawyer was glad Bud only worked part-time since he didn't put much effort into the chores. Still, it was an extra pair of hands, and Sawyer couldn't imagine trying to do everything himself.

He left the pole barn and strode toward the steer corral. Frowned as he saw the UTV parked on the other side with no one in it. Was Bud still here? Had something happened?

A flash of worry hit him. He took off at a jog and quickly checked around for signs of Bud. Nothing. The smell of cattle and manure and fresh winter air swirled as he walked past the buildings to where Bud usually parked. His truck wasn't there.

Frustration mounted as Sawyer stomped back to the UTV. The key was in it. Shaking his head, he started it up and drove it back to the pole barn. If Bud couldn't—or wouldn't—do the simple task of returning the UTV where it belonged, was he worth keeping on as an employee?

Sawyer took a minute to sweep up the dirt it had dragged in, then headed to the ranch office.

The light was on. Maybe Tess had decided to come out early.

He paused in the doorway. Ken sat behind the desk, pen in hand, studying the daily ledgers Sawyer had kept since arriving. The man coughed, and the harshness of it brought a pain to Sawyer's own chest. Someone in his condition shouldn't be out in this cold. It was always harder to breathe in frigid air.

"Good afternoon, Ken." Sawyer pulled up a chair. "What brings you out here?"

"Eh." The man gave a flick of the pen. "I've got no use for sitting around in the house. I got cattle depending on me."

Wasn't that why Ken was paying him to manage the place? Ken had specifically hired him because he was retiring.

Had Bud or Tess complained about the job he was doing?

Maybe the man was just restless. Sawyer couldn't imagine being stuck inside for weeks on end.

"Well, it's good to see you're feeling better." He gestured to the ledgers. "If you have any questions…"

Ken looked up. His eyes were clear. But another cough racked his bony frame. It took everything in Sawyer not to insist he go back inside. Protect his lungs.

"You're underfeeding the cattle." Ken sat back, straightening, and gave him a shrewd look.

"Why do you say that?" A burning sensation spread through his chest. After all he'd done for the ranch, Ken still didn't trust him. Sawyer would never hurt the cattle to save a few bucks.

He pointed to the ledger. "It's right here in your own handwriting. By my calculations, you're off by almost fifteen percent. I didn't hire you to starve my cows."

Sawyer shifted the chair closer to the desk. Then he traced his finger down the column where he logged each day's hay. "I'm feeding less because there's less waste. After I spread the line of hay, I measure it. If the conditions aren't muddy, I come back and rake the remainder. Now that I know how much they actually eat, I don't give them as much."

"Humph." Ken stared at him through narrow eyes for a long moment. "Bud told me you're nitpicking him to death."

Wow. He had no idea how to respond to that one. He wanted to nitpick the guy, but usually he simply instructed Bud to redo the chores he carelessly performed. Sawyer picked up the slack on everything else.

"Bud and I don't see eye to eye on how chores should be done."

"I don't care how the stalls are mucked, son." Ken

made a sucking sound with his teeth. "I just care that they're clean."

"Then you and I are on the same page. You hired me to manage this place, and I'm not going to let sloppy work get a pass."

A stretch of silence tied Sawyer's gut into a knot. From everything Tess had told him, the ranch was near the financial edge. And he'd taken a big pay cut and was working after hours to get it back on its feet. To be scolded by the owner he was sacrificing for was too much.

He might as well bring up selling the equipment while he had Ken here. At this point, he had nothing to lose.

"I've been looking for ways to streamline the ranch. I'm in the process of taking inventory of the outbuildings. There's an old tractor I think we could fix up and sell."

"Sell?" Ken tossed the pen on the desk and glared at him. "The only things we sell around here are calves, got it?"

"Look, Tess mentioned cash-flow issues. The newer tractor already does everything the old one would do. You don't need both."

"It doesn't do everything. I use the other tractor for scraping out the corrals."

"If we attach the box blade to the new tractor, we can scrape the corrals out and do cleanup with the Bobcat."

"Won't fit." Ken's cheeks grew red. "The new tractor is too big."

"Both tractors are the same length." Why was Ken arguing? He doubted they could get the other one started anyhow.

"We might need it."

"Does the old one even work?"

Ken opened his mouth and closed it. Then he mumbled something Sawyer didn't catch.

Tess, carrying Tucker, appeared in the doorway. "Daddy, you know better than to come out here on a day like this."

"What? I'm inside." He had the look of a thief caught red-handed.

"It's too cold."

"Papa!" Tucker wiggled until Tess set him down. Then he ran around the desk and held up his arms for Ken to pick him up. Ken settled him on his lap.

"See? We're good here." Ken didn't meet her eyes.

Sawyer wasn't getting involved. Besides, he couldn't tear his gaze away from her pretty face. He could tell she was weighing her options—insist her dad return to the house at once or indulge him for a little while?

"You've got thirty minutes, mister." She pointed to her father, then turned to Sawyer. "Do you have a minute?"

She wanted to talk to him? About what? His nerves jangled like the jingle bells on every television commercial lately. First, Ken basically accused him of mismanaging the ranch, and now Tess had something to discuss?

"Sure." He rose.

"Leave Tuck with me," Ken said gruffly.

"Okay. We won't be long." She eased away from the doorway and Sawyer joined her.

"What's up?"

She didn't answer, just strode toward the door.

Was she mad at him about something? What if she, too, accused him of not doing a good job? Did she blame him for her dad coming out today?

Out in the fresh air, she slowed. When she reached the fence where the horses were turned out, she faced him with a radiant smile. It chased away every question in his mind.

He had an uneasy sensation he'd agree to about anything if it would make her happy. He gulped. *Please, God, don't let her ask me to give up any more than I already have.*

Tess had been waiting all morning to share her good news. She was taking his suggestion and starting her own freelance bookkeeping service. But one look at Sawyer's face and she knew something was wrong. Her own happiness collapsed under an onslaught of fresh worries.

"What did Daddy say? Something happened, didn't it?"

"I was surprised to see him out here."

"Yeah, well, I'm surprised I could keep him in the house as long as I did." She tried to make light of it, but didn't quite succeed.

"He doesn't seem to think my feeding strategy is wise."

"Why not?" She'd been over the numbers with Sawyer and was impressed at the amount of hay he was conserving.

He shrugged. "Thinks I'm starving the cattle."

"Did you explain about the waste?"

"I did."

"What else?" Daddy had been grouchy all weekend. His energy was returning, and with it the edgy restlessness he only knew how to deal with by saddling up and riding out. Which she had forbidden.

"Apparently Bud thinks I'm too nitpicky."

"Did you tell him to open his eyes? This place has

never looked so good. Nitpicky makes a difference," she scoffed, shaking her head.

A hint of a smile flitted on Sawyer's lips. Then he leaned his forearms against the top rail of the fence and watched her horse, Rocky, toss his head near Pansy, while the other horses flicked their tails nearby.

"There's an old tractor in the outbuilding." He pointed to the left, where a row of old sheds stood. "You don't need it. The new tractor functions the same. You could fix it and sell it. It would stretch the money another month or two."

Understanding chased away her anxiety. "Oh, I get it. That's what got Daddy riled up. And that's why you're upset."

"I'm not upset."

"I've been around cowboys long enough to know when something's wrong." She reached over and laid her gloved hand on his arm, strong beneath his winter jacket. "It's okay to admit it. Anyone who works with my father is bound to get annoyed at some point. I know I do all the time."

Sawyer shifted then, facing her. His blue eyes trapped her gaze, and a sense of anticipation filled her.

"Do you trust me?" he asked quietly.

"Yes." She hadn't expected the question.

"The cattle are important to me. You know that, right?"

"I know." Where was he coming from? Why all this intensity?

"When I told you I'd find ways to make this place profitable, I assumed you knew I wouldn't do it at the expense of the herd."

"You assumed correctly." A blast of wind chilled the

skin below her collar. She drew her shoulders up and wrapped her coat more tightly around her body.

"I told your father that I was reducing waste. I don't just go doing whatever I feel like." If his eyebrows dipped any lower, he'd have a unibrow.

"Is something wrong? What are you saying?"

"No, nothing's wrong." He stared off in the distance as if he were trying to convince himself of the fact.

"Well, good." The cold seeped right through her layers. She'd best tell him what she'd come out here to say before she froze to death. "I've decided to take your advice. Last night, I spent hours researching. I'm going to start my own freelance bookkeeping service."

In the beat that followed, she could hear echoes of Devin's voice in her mind. *Whatever you want, babe.* Her ex had barely listened to her. Had placated her by agreeing with her plans until they inconvenienced him. If Sawyer brushed this off with a lukewarm *that's nice,* she'd be hurt.

"Wow, you're really doing it." His mouth curved into a big grin. "You'll be great. Is there anything I can do to help?"

His words warmed her more than a crackling fire in the fireplace ever could.

"You already did. Thanks for giving me the idea. I'm a little nervous. I've never done this for other people."

"I didn't have anything to do with it." His cheeks flushed and he turned his attention to his boots. "With the way you understand the ranch's finances, you'll be a natural. You're going to have more work than you know what to do with."

While she could use the money, between keeping up

with a very busy two-year-old and a very stubborn father, she worried about finding the time to do a good job.

"I'll be happy with a few clients to start." She hitched her head back toward the pole barn. "Should we head back?"

"That was what you wanted to talk to me about?" His expression questioned, probed her.

"Yeah. I, well, I wouldn't have thought of starting my own business if it weren't for you. I figured you'd want to know." Maybe she shouldn't have cornered him. Sharing and friendship could easily jump the fence to become more. If there was one thing she couldn't afford at this point in her life, it was another doomed relationship.

He stepped toward her, and before she registered what was happening, he wrapped her in a hug.

"Congratulations. You'll be great." He stepped back and stared into her eyes.

"Thanks." Those strong arms could be addictive. But even more addictive could be his emotional support.

"What do you have to do to begin?"

As they strolled back to the pole barn, she told him about deciding on a company name, registering with the state, filing for an employer identification number and setting up a business account with the bank. He listened, nodding now and again. When she finished, she tipped her head back. "There's so much to do, but I already have a lot of it underway."

"I can't believe you got all that figured out in one night." He stopped at the door.

It was the first time in years she was this full of hope and excitement. And Sawyer had let her share it with him, even after a hard meeting with her dad.

She hadn't told Daddy about Sawyer's cut in pay. Hadn't wanted to kick up a hornet's nest with him feeling so sick. But if her father knew Sawyer had a personal stake in improving the ranch's finances, he might not be so quick to condemn the new way of doing things. Maybe he'd even warm to the idea of selling the tractor Sawyer mentioned. What other equipment was sitting around gathering dust when it could be making them money?

Her cell phone rang. "Go on without me. I'll be there in a minute."

He nodded and continued on inside.

She answered the phone and was surprised to find out her car was already fixed. She thanked the man and ended the call.

If things kept improving at this rate, it would be her best Christmas in recent memories. And she sincerely hoped it would be. They could all use a healthy dose of holiday cheer.

An hour later, Sawyer glanced at Tess sitting in the passenger seat as he drove her to town. Her profile revealed a slight smile as she stared out at the scenery. Good. She deserved some serenity with all that was going on.

When Sawyer had returned to the office, Ken pushed himself out of the chair and announced he needed a cup of coffee. Then Tess had appeared in the doorway with the news her car was fixed. Naturally, Sawyer offered to take her into town to pick it up. Ken said he'd watch Tucker for her.

It had all happened so quickly, he'd forgotten he'd been planning on repairing shingles on one of the sheds today.

Too late now.

An uneasy feeling crawled under his skin. Was he letting Ken and Tess take advantage of him?

Nonsense. He was the one who'd offered to take a pay cut and find ways to cut costs. He was the one who'd insisted on driving Tess into town to get her car. But was he offering too much and getting too little in return?

Was he willingly making himself a doormat for everyone on this ranch? Didn't take a genius to see Bud was walking all over him in the chore department. The UTV being left outside earlier made his blood boil. And then when Ken accused him of starving the cattle? He would never mistreat the herd. The conversation had lasered warning signals to his very core.

He couldn't afford to have his trust crushed again.

Maybe he was worrying over nothing. When Ken saw the wisdom of his suggestions, the ranch would be profitable. Sawyer would still be the manager. His pay would be reinstated. He'd save for the house outside of town. Spend time with his friends. Guard his heart the way he should.

When Tess had shared her new business plan, he'd hung on every word. She lit up when she was excited. And he could sense the nerves, the doubts beneath her no-nonsense exterior. He liked being the one she confided in.

She'd be successful. He didn't doubt it for a minute.

Another reason he should distance himself from her more. What did a washed-up cowboy like him have to offer her?

"I was thinking about stopping in at Dino's and ordering a pizza for dinner." Tess looked at him as if expecting a response.

"Okay."

"Do you mind stopping there before we get my car? That way it'll be ready by the time I finish at the auto shop."

"Sure." That word summed up his life. *Sure.*

Why did he agree to everything? Maybe he didn't have time to stop in at the pizza joint in addition to the auto shop. Did anyone think of that?

"Unless you're too busy." Her pretty eyes shimmered. "It's so nice of you to do this for me. I don't want you to think I'm taking advantage of you. Why don't you eat with us tonight?"

Shame hit him hard. Tess wasn't taking advantage of him. Her dad? Bud? Yes, but not Tess.

"I'll stop at Dino's first. You don't have to invite me to supper."

"Have to? I want to. In case you missed it, I share meals with a very messy toddler and one ornery cooped-up rancher. It's nice when you're around."

He swallowed, gripping the wheel tightly. She liked having him around? Her words weren't helping him with the whole guarding-his-heart-and-putting-distance-between-them thing.

Falling for the boss's daughter would be even dumber than adding Christina to his bank accounts had been.

He was older, wiser now.

"I'll have to pass this time. I'm, uh, busy." He had a hot list a mile long to tackle back at the ranch. Sharing a pizza with her and Tucker and Ken sounded great, though. He'd gotten wrapped up in her little world, and he liked being in it. He wanted to be the one she leaned on.

The same as he'd wanted with Christina.

"If you change your mind…" Her shoulder lifted in a small shrug as she gazed out the window again.

The miles passed and they reached the outskirts of town.

"I've been thinking about what you told me earlier," she said. "About selling the tractor."

"Oh, yeah?" He turned at the intersection, tempted to tell her he wanted to eat with her after all.

"Yeah. If you can't convince Daddy to sell it, maybe we could rent it out from time to time."

He mulled on it as other possibilities blossomed.

"Has anyone ever told you you're really smart?" He shot her a grin.

"Only you."

"Well, you are." He parked his truck in front of the pizza place. "That's a good idea."

"I have my moments." She grinned and hopped out. "I'll be back in a minute."

He needed to stop comparing Tess to Christina. Tess genuinely cared about the ranch, her father and her son. Christina had only cared about herself.

It didn't matter if the women were polar opposites, though.

It only mattered that he was still the same old Sawyer. He didn't have a future with Tess. Couldn't. He had goals, modest as they were, and if he fooled himself into losing sight of them to help her and her father, he'd never get the little house outside of town. He'd lose what self-respect he'd scraped together.

The sooner he got it through his thick skull Tess and her boy were off-limits, the better.

Chapter Seven

By Friday morning, Sawyer had had it up to here dealing with Bud's laziness. Christmas was only a few weeks away, and it was time to insist the man pull his weight and do his job right.

His insubordination had been gnawing at him all week. Sawyer had been ignoring a lot of the problems, redoing most of the chores, and he'd told Bud more than once he expected better work out of him. A good manager looked out for the business, and he had a duty to make sure the employees were doing things right.

Unfortunately, nothing was working. Including Bud.

Speaking of... Bud lumbered into the pole barn. Sawyer checked the time. It was an hour before Bud's workday ended. Sawyer had just finished checking cattle and was getting ready to determine the rest of the day's work. He scanned the list of chores on the whiteboard.

"Did you check the water tank in the south pasture?" Sawyer asked.

Bud glared at him and didn't answer. Normally, Sawyer would let it go, but not anymore.

"What's wrong?" Sawyer asked. "Didn't you hear me?"

"I heard you, and *yes*, I checked. It's fine." He scratched his beard. "I'll get the straw down for the steers before I take off."

"It's only eleven." It didn't take an hour to give the steers new straw.

"Yeah, so?" He put his hands on his hips.

"Your day ends at noon."

"What's your point? It takes a while to spread the straw."

Was this guy being serious? Sawyer ground his teeth together and turned his attention to the whiteboard. One of the items was swapping out the damaged ring feeder in the bull pasture for a new one. He'd had more pressing tasks to attend to all week, so it still needed to be replaced.

"After you're done with the straw, I need you to take the new ring feeder to the bull pasture. Swap out the old one."

"Won't have time." The man eased his body into the driver's seat of the Bobcat and started it up. The noise of the engine made it impossible to talk. In three strides, Sawyer was next to Bud.

"You waste a lot of time," he yelled over the engine.

"What?" He gunned the accelerator to make it louder.

"Turn that off." Sawyer pointed to the ignition.

"Seems to me you're the one wasting time." He pointed to the tractor, then the door. "What's the boss going to think about you neglecting the cows to put up wreaths around here?" Then Bud gave him a sarcastic smile, wriggled his fingers and backed the vehicle out of the pole barn.

He couldn't believe the lack of respect this guy had for him. Yeah, Sawyer had ridden out to the forest and cut weeping spruce branches to hang as boughs over the office door. He'd also made homemade wreaths of juniper and hung them over the exterior doors of the pole barn and stables. But he'd done it on his own time.

The one he'd placed on the front of the tractor had been for Tucker. He'd known the boy would love it, and he was right. Tuck had squealed when he saw it. For Bud to suggest he was neglecting his duties was the ultimate insult.

Sawyer loped to the steer corral and waited by the gate. A full ten minutes later, Bud drove the Bobcat loaded with straw to the corral. He waved for Sawyer to open the gate.

Sawyer widened his stance, crossed his arms over his chest and stood his ground.

Narrowing his eyes, Bud hitched his chin. Then he shifted the loader to drop the bales inches from Sawyer's feet. He backed up the Bobcat and took off in a cloud of dirty exhaust.

Sawyer debated his next move. It was more than likely Bud was getting another bale of straw and would be back momentarily. Whether he was or not, they had to discuss this.

The blatant disrespect was ending. Today.

Although his nose was frozen and his fingers grew icy under his work gloves, he didn't move an inch. Bud probably thought Sawyer would haul the hay into the corral and spread it out under the shed. Normally, he would.

Anger burned in his chest. The more he thought about it, the tenser he got. He checked his phone.

Ten minutes passed.

Fifteen.

It should take roughly two minutes to load a bale of hay on the front loader and drive the machine back here.

What was Bud doing?

The rumble of the engine approached, and Bud smirked as he pulled up in front of Sawyer. The bale dropped on top of the other one. Bud yelled out, "There you go."

"Get out here and deal with this."

"You're blocking the gate."

Sawyer stormed up to the Bobcat and got in Bud's face. "Get out. Deal with this." Every word landed like a knife sinking into a bull's-eye.

With a sour expression, Bud hefted himself out. Then he went into the corral, let the steers out through the other gate, tossed each bale inside and carried one over to the open shed where the steers slept. He cut open the bales and left them the way they were, then trekked back to Sawyer with a nasty gleam in his eye.

"There. Finished."

"You didn't spread out the straw. You haven't let the steers back in." He stood stiff, furious. "Go back."

"They'll toss it around. They always do." Bud tried to brush past him.

"I told you to go back. Spread the straw. Let the steers back in." His tone was so harsh he wasn't sure where it came from.

Bud sized him up and down, gave a contemptuous snort and complied. Then he glared at Sawyer as he got back in the Bobcat and drove away.

The steers always got excited with new straw, and Sawyer took a few minutes to watch them frolic and leap around. Watching them took the edge off his anger, and soon the only emotion lingering was resignation.

He couldn't work with Bud anymore. He'd talk to Ken this afternoon about firing him and hiring someone else.

In the meantime, he had a lot of work to do.

"Do you have a minute?" Late Friday afternoon, Tess poked her head into her father's room after knocking. "I've been meaning to discuss something with you."

He was sitting up in his bed, glasses on, scribbling something on a notepad. He wore gray sweatpants and a Wyoming Cowboys sweatshirt, so he must be feeling better. On his bad days, he stayed in pajamas. This entire week had been a string of bad days. Her heart ached for him. It seemed as soon as he had a good stretch, he had a bad one twice as long. It was tough on him, and it was tough on her, too.

But since he seemed to be doing okay, she figured she could finally tell him about Sawyer voluntarily taking a pay cut to help out.

"What's on your mind, Tessie-girl?" He smiled, setting aside the notepad.

She padded over to the chair next to his bed. "You doing okay? You need anything?"

"I'm fine. What did you want to talk about?"

"The finances—"

"I don't want to hear another word about selling land or tractors or cashing in an IRA." He waved his index finger.

"I know, Daddy. That's not why I'm here."

He gave her a skeptical glance.

"Back on Thanksgiving, I went over to Sawyer's. I was honest with him about the ranch having cash-flow problems. I didn't tell you because you were having a rough go with the chemo."

"Why would you do that? It's none of his business. It's *my* business."

She'd expected the outburst and calmly continued, "At the time, he offered to take a big cut in pay—a temporary one—and assured me he'd find ways to cut costs and bring in more income."

"By starving the cows." He picked up the notepad just to slap it against his leg. "And selling my equipment."

"He's not starving the cows." She wanted to shake him. The man exasperated her to no end. "He's doing a good job, Daddy. He works really hard. And he's doing it for next to nothing. So please don't accuse him of hurting the ranch. He's helping us."

From the set of his jaw and the way his lips were pursed, she could tell there was no getting through to him at the moment. He'd need some time to process what she'd said.

"I'm taking Tucker to the Christmas parade tomorrow. I plan on handing out flyers to advertise my bookkeeping business."

"I told you not to work—"

"And I told you I'm doing this for me." She took his hand in hers. "I need this, Daddy. Can't you be happy for me?"

The bluster deflated from him. "I'm not going to be bedridden forever, Tess. I'm taking care of this ranch and you and Tucker."

"I know, Daddy." She squeezed his hand. "You've always taken care of me. You do a good job of it. But now it's my job to take care of Tucker."

His face softened. "He'll like the parade. Do they still throw out candy?"

"I'm sure they do. If you're up to it, you can join us. I can find you a spot in the coffee shop, where it's warm."

"I appreciate it, but if I'm feeling good, I'm checking on the cattle. It's been too long since I've been out there."

"No." How could he even think about riding out and checking cattle in the middle of December when he'd been too sick to get out of bed three of the past four days? "It's too cold. Bad for your lungs. You need to stay inside, where it's warm."

He pushed his glasses up higher on his nose and gave her the look. She took it as her cue to get out. Rising, she mentally calculated if he needed anything. He still had half a glass of water. Fresh box of tissues. Medicine, television remote and extra pillows were all there.

"Supper will be in an hour." She left the room, softly shutting the door behind her. She paused in the hall, questioning the wisdom of telling him about Sawyer and arguing with him about her business.

How much longer would she have him around? Pressure built behind her eyes. They'd been arguing since she could remember. It was their preferred method of communicating. The day she stopped arguing with him would be the day his health plummeted to the point of no return, and she tried not to think about it.

She didn't think she'd be able to handle it when he passed away. A world without her daddy didn't make sense.

A tear slipped down her cheek. Then another. And she forced her feet forward as she swiped the tears away. In the living room, Tucker rubbed his eyes as he woke from his nap. Tufts of his brown hair stood on end, and he raised chubby arms over his head for her to pick him up. "Mama."

She hoisted him in her arms, kissing his cheek and holding him close. Ladybug stretched on the rug where she'd been lying and ambled over, wagging her tail.

"You woke up." She looked into her son's precious brown eyes and almost started crying again. Christmas was coming soon, and she wanted it to be special for him. Last year, he'd played more with the wrapping paper than with his actual gifts. But now that he was two, he had a better understanding of things. She'd ordered him an inflatable plastic ball pit for toddlers. It even had a little slide. Perfect for long, cold Wyoming winters where they spent more time indoors than out.

Every afternoon this week, he'd begged to see *Soy* and she'd happily taken him with her to see Sawyer. She'd laughed when she saw the wreath on the tractor. Tucker's mouth had formed an O, and he'd bounced and clapped and pointed at the *twac, twac* until Sawyer lifted him up to inspect the wreath himself. When Sawyer said, "Ho, ho, ho," in a burly tone, Tucker proceeded to copy him. The child now referred to every Christmas decoration in the house as *ho, ho*.

"Me firsty, Mama." He clutched two fistfuls of her long hair and wiped them on his cheeks. "Soft."

"I'm glad you like my hair, bud. Let's get you some milk."

Carrying him to the kitchen, she shifted him to one hip and opened the fridge. Pulling out a half gallon of milk, she set him on his feet so she could prepare a sippy cup for him. A knock at the front door put the giddy-up in her go. Once she'd poured the milk and screwed on the top, she handed the cup to Tucker and hustled to the door with him and Ladybug at her heels.

Sawyer stood on the doorstep. He'd changed out of

his work clothes into jeans and a sweatshirt under his unzipped coat. He smelled fresh, like pine and spices.

"Come in." She ushered him into the hall. "What's going on?"

"I'm here to talk to Ken." He took off his cowboy hat and held it between his hands. Tucker attached himself to Sawyer's leg, sipped his milk and looked up at him. Sawyer hoisted him into his arms. "Hey, Tuck. What you got there?"

He laid his cheek against Sawyer's shoulder and kept drinking.

"He just woke up." Tess gestured for him to follow her and stopped at the kitchen counter, where stacks of papers she'd printed earlier loomed. "Daddy's in his room. You can head on back."

Sawyer paused near the first stack and peered at the top. "What's this?"

"Oh, I made up some flyers to advertise my bookkeeping services. I'm handing them out tomorrow after the Christmas parade."

He nodded, a nostalgic look on his face. "I forgot about the parade. It was always a big deal when we were growing up."

"I want to make it a tradition for Tucker. I think he's going to love it."

"What's not to love about floats and Christmas music and candy, right?" Sawyer looked so natural holding her son in his arms that she had to look away. He never hesitated to love on Tucker.

Devin hadn't held him in months.

She began organizing the stacks of flyers, alternating the piles between different colors.

"Who's going to watch this little guy while you pass out the flyers and talk to the store owners?"

She hadn't thought about the logistics of actually handing them out tomorrow. Keeping track of Tucker kept her hands full most days. Hannah would be watching the parade with her nieces and nephews and wouldn't be able to give Tess a hand. She could call one of her other friends, but she hated to ask them so last-minute.

"I haven't thought that far ahead."

"What time's the parade?" he asked.

"Eleven."

"When do you plan on heading home?"

"After I hand out the flyers. Why?"

"Well, I could come with you and take care of Tuck while you get the word out about your business. Then you wouldn't have to worry about watching him. You can focus on what needs to be done."

"You'd do that?" Her hands dropped to her sides and she angled her head to look at him.

Sometimes Sawyer was too good to be true.

"Yeah, of course." He looked taken aback.

"Well, I'm taking you up on your offer, then."

"Good. I have to get back in the afternoon, though, to finish chores."

"Not a problem. I'll be more than ready to recover from the excitement anyhow. And this one will need a nap."

"No nap." Tucker held out his sippy cup and scowled.

"We'll both take a nap. We'll snuggle. How's that sound?"

"Twac, twac, Soy?" Tuck ignored her, turning hopeful eyes to Sawyer. "Ho, ho?"

"No tractor today, buddy." Sawyer handed him to her. "I have to talk to your grandpa."

"Papa?"

"Yep."

Sawyer winked at him and patted Ladybug's head. "I better get in there."

Tess watched him walk down the hall and heard him knock on Daddy's door. Then their voices were too muffled to hear what they were talking about. She set Tucker back on his feet and went to the closet to find something to put all the flyers in. A red-plaid canvas tote and several other bags were stuffed behind rolls of paper towels.

The plaid was festive, Christmassy. Perfect.

Ever since he'd arrived, Sawyer had helped her keep her life together. She hadn't gotten him a gift yet. She'd think of something nice for him—after all, he'd given her hope. The best Christmas gift of all.

"How are you doing?" Sawyer sat in the chair next to Ken's bed. The man looked healthy—sharp, even. Good. Sawyer needed to tell him about Bud, and the conversation would go better if Ken wasn't feeling sick.

"I'm great." Ken had a self-satisfied air about him.

"You look well."

"And it's a good thing, too." Ken skewered him with a piercing stare. "Bud quit."

"He quit?" Well, at least Sawyer wouldn't have to fire him.

"Yes, and he had a lot to say about it."

He tensed. Of course he did. And no doubt Ken believed every word Bud said.

When would he ever get the benefit of the doubt? This side of never, most likely.

He remained calm, keeping eye contact with the man. He had nothing to feel guilty about. "I'll call around and see if anyone's looking for part-time work. We shouldn't have any trouble replacing him."

"I'm not replacing him." Ken's legs were stretched out on top of the quilt, and he crossed one ankle over the other, as calm as could be.

"What?" His brain scrambled, thinking of how much extra work it would mean for him.

"Tess told you the truth when she said the ranch is going through a tough phase. I can't afford to hire someone else."

Had Tess told her father he'd taken a huge pay cut? Did it even matter at this point?

"With all due respect, this ranch is a lot for one person to handle."

"You saying you can't handle it?"

"No." *Yes.* He'd been caught between a rock and a hard place before, but this felt extra tight.

"Good. I'm counting on you. Tess is counting on you. Tucker's counting on you." He inhaled deeply, not coughing for once. "I'll be out to help as soon as I'm able."

Sawyer wanted to drop his forehead into his hands, but he didn't. Was Ken out of touch with reality? The man was sick. Being outdoors in this weather wasn't good for him. Days out in the brittle cold would tax his lungs. And yet he was planning on working?

"What about retiring?" Sawyer asked. "I'd hate to see your health take a dive when you're on the verge of enjoying some free time."

"Bah." He waved in an offhand manner. "I've got all the time in the world right now, and it's boring. I'll be ready to saddle up soon."

"Does Tess know?"

"I don't need permission to ride around this ranch, son. Don't forget it."

Okay, then.

"The ranch will run better with another cowboy. How about I ask around for a part-time hand until you're feeling up to it?"

"I don't think you got my message." Ken shifted his jaw. "There will be no part-timer."

The silence in the room grew oppressive. "I understand. I'll see myself out."

He rose and left the room, not looking back.

Double the work. Half the pay.

Ken was right about one thing. The ranch and all who lived on it were counting on Sawyer right now. Although the situation was unfair to him, he couldn't leave a sick man, a single mom and a little boy in the lurch. Especially not before Christmas.

It just wasn't who he was.

Chapter Eight

Why wasn't she enjoying the parade?

Tess propped a smile on her face as another float went by and, waving flags, several teens on horseback trotted behind it. Parade marchers tossed candy to the kiddos. Everyone was bundled up for winter. The entire town had turned out, and Tucker was having the time of his life. At least one of them was. She couldn't stop worrying about Daddy. Yesterday, she'd figured he was bluffing when he mentioned checking cattle, but this morning he'd made a hearty bowl of oatmeal and put on a pair of jeans and a flannel shirt.

He wasn't seriously going out riding today, was he?

No, he wasn't foolish. Temperamental and impatient, yes, but not dumb. He'd stay inside.

She hoped.

A group of carolers singing "We Wish You a Merry Christmas" sauntered past. Coming to the annual Sunrise Bend Christmas parade would be a tradition from now on. One of many new traditions. And she'd actually enjoy them next year. This year, her mind was too muddled.

She still wasn't sure how the holidays would play out with her ex.

Tess had left several messages for Devin to call her back so they could iron out their Christmas plans. If it meant she had to drive down to Laramie so Tuck could see his father and grandparents, she would. The boy might not have a dad in his everyday life, but she'd do her best to make sure he stayed connected with Devin. In the meantime, she'd give him other things to look forward to, including this.

Maybe her sweet boy would be one of those teens on horseback someday. The thought made her heart glow.

Near the curb, Sawyer kept his hands firm on Tucker's shoulders. The two of them had been scrambling for candy ever since the parade began. A few more minutes and it would be over. The red-plaid tote full of flyers sitting at her feet gave her a fresh case of nerves.

Would anyone be interested in hiring her? What if all her work was for nothing?

As the final float with Santa and his reindeer drove by, Tucker yelled, "Ho, ho!"

She and Sawyer laughed. He picked up Tucker and gave her an expectant look as the crowd began to disperse. "Where to first?"

Her phone chimed. *Please, Lord, don't let it be Daddy. Only You can keep him from pushing himself too hard.*

She quickly checked it. A text from Devin appeared on the screen. I'm swamped with holiday parties at the restaurants. It will have to wait.

Anger bubbled up deep in her core. *It?* Was that what he considered his son? An object, a situation? Her baby deserved better.

Her thumbs flew into overdrive. I'll drive there if necessary. Would a weekday work?

Feeling ragey, she texted again. He's your son.

"Tess?"

Her blurred vision snapped back into focus. Tucker clutched two fistfuls of candy and was babbling something in Sawyer's ear. Regrets threatened to overtake her.

She'd been looking forward to the parade, and all she'd done was worry about Daddy. Now she was letting Devin's selfishness ruin her mood. What was wrong with her?

Forcing a chipper expression on her face, she pulled back her shoulders and clutched the tote strap. "Let's get the wagon, then start at the first store on the end of the street. We'll work our way down, cross over, and then I'll pop into the businesses on the side streets."

"Sounds good." He fell in next to her as they jostled through the crowd toward his truck. He handed Tucker to her and took out the red wagon from the back. The toddler hated sitting in a stroller but loved riding in the wagon.

Tess lined a fleece blanket on the bottom of the wagon, set Tucker on top of it and spread another soft blanket across his lap. He clapped his hands, then bunched both fists in the material, drawing it up to his chin with a grin. "Go!"

"You ready, buddy?" Sawyer took the handle and started pulling as Tucker yelled, "Whee!"

The crowd was thinning out, so they had an easy time getting to the insurance agency on the corner. All the businesses were open today for a special Christmas open house. Bells clanged as doors opened.

"I'll wait out here with Tuck." Sawyer nodded to the wagon. "Do your thing."

"Thanks, Sawyer." A case of the nerves struck her full force, and she pivoted so he wouldn't see. *Come on—be strong. For your son. You can do this.*

Could she, though? Or was this freelancing idea just a fantasy like her other dreams had been? Would she be dismissed the way she'd been for years with Devin?

Only one way to find out.

She took a deep breath, opened the door and went inside. The small reception area had a Christmas tree in the corner and silver garlands draped in front of the desks. An instrumental version of "Greensleeves" played. She approached the front desk, where coffee and cookies had been set out in honor of the open house. It smelled delicious in here.

"Hi, Simone. When did you start working here?" She recognized the bubbly dark-skinned beauty with bouncy curls from church.

"Just hired in last month." Simone smiled. "Where's your boy? I could use a dose of his cuteness right now."

"He's outside with Sawyer."

"Sawyer, huh? I saw him in church last week." Simone craned her neck toward the front window. "Why didn't you bring that hunk in here?"

"He's doing me a favor today, helping with Tuck." Sawyer was more than a hunk. He was a true friend. A fine-looking friend. Reaching into the tote, she pulled out a flyer and passed it to her. "I'm starting a bookkeeping service. I don't know who takes care of the finances here, but I can help you out with any of your needs, big or small."

"That's Ray. He takes care of the billing." Simone

scanned the sheet. "I'll give this to him. Say, do you have any more of these?"

"I have a ton," she admitted with a nervous shrug.

"Why don't you leave a few? That way if anyone comes in, they can take one."

"Really? You wouldn't mind?" She took out a small stack of the flyers and handed them over. "I appreciate this. If there's anything I can do for you, let me know."

"It's no problem. I hope you get lots of calls."

"Thanks. I do, too." Tess waved goodbye and left.

Finally, something in her life she wasn't at the mercy of her father's or husband's whims about. It had been a long time since she'd had any real control over her life. This business was a start. And she had Sawyer to thank for it.

They'd made their way down one side of the street when the allure of the wagon wore off for Tucker. Sawyer was surprised the boy had stayed in there as long as he had. He'd been on the verge of a tantrum for a while.

"Walk, Mama," he said over and over, pounding his mittened fists on the side of the wagon.

"Not yet, baby." Tess glowed beside him. She was getting a warm reception from the area businesses. Two owners already told her they'd be in touch soon. He liked seeing her happy. He hadn't realized how unusual it was to see her smile so freely.

"Walk!" He kicked his little boots in the wagon.

Sawyer shot Tess a questioning glance. "Why don't we take a break. Get some *c-o-c-o-a*?"

"Yeah, I could use a *c-o-f-f-e-e*." She nudged her elbow into his side and grinned.

"Sounds good."

They continued up the block to the coffee shop. Sawyer had been keeping track of the time. He needed to head back in another hour to check the cows again, but he'd been enjoying this outing with her and Tucker so much he didn't mind delaying it a bit.

Last night, he'd gone over the daily checklist of chores he'd been splitting with Bud. He'd been doing about three-quarters of them on his own and redoing some of the others. Not having the extra help would be a challenge, but if he worked a few extra hours each day, he should be able to handle it.

He didn't want to, though. It wasn't what he'd signed up for.

They reached the coffee shop. White Christmas lights wrapped in green garland twinkled from inside the large front window.

"Let's leave the wagon out here." Sawyer wheeled it snug to the building and took Tucker out, setting him on his feet. "It should be fine. It's not supposed to snow until later."

"You want a cookie and chocolate milk?" Tess bent down to look in the boy's eyes.

"Cookie!" His entire face lit up. Tess took his hand and led the boy inside with Sawyer behind them.

After they ordered, they snagged a table someone had just left. The place was packed. "Rudolph the Red-Nosed Reindeer" played, conversation hummed and loud peals of laughter erupted now and then.

Tess unzipped Tucker's snowsuit and took off his hat and mittens, then settled him in a wooden high chair and handed him his cookie and milk. Closing her eyes, she massaged the back of her neck.

Sawyer wanted to reach over and massage it for her.

Touch that silky hair. Work out the knots in her stressed-out muscles.

He lunged for his coffee and took a sip. Steaming hot. Maybe if he burned his tongue it would take his mind off touching Tess.

Yeah, right. All day he'd been basking in the Christmas spirit. Had enjoyed walking by her side, helping out with her son, being the one she smiled at when she came back out after dropping off another flyer. He'd stopped and chatted with people he hadn't seen in years. And it had felt right.

He liked Tess.

A lot.

Too much.

"Oh, while I'm here, I'd better give them a flyer." Tess's eyes blinked open and she took out a small stack. "I'll be right back."

He tracked her progress through the crowded tables to the end of the long line. She'd be a while. A sense of having done this before came over him. He remembered sitting at a table in a crowded bar in New York City while Christina chatted up the owner. She'd tried to convince the guy to book her to sing. Sawyer had leaned back in his chair and watched her smiling, flirting, doing whatever it took to get the gig. Then she'd confidently made her way back to him and told him she'd gotten it.

He'd waited until they were out on the sidewalk to hug her off her feet. She immediately launched into a list of all the things she'd need—outfits, posters, advertising—and he'd been proud of her. Been proud to be the guy she chose to be her boyfriend.

A raspy voice behind him brought him back to the present. "Bud said that Roth kid was running it into the ground and that's why he quit. Ken should have known better than to trust him."

Sawyer stiffened. Kid? He was too old to be put in that category anymore.

"And now he's playing patty-cake with Ken's grandson and his daughter. It's obvious what's going on."

"What do you mean?" a low male voice asked.

"He wants the ranch back. And he's preying on the daughter to make it happen."

A trio of older ladies entered the shop, all talking loudly, so Sawyer missed what the men said next. He sensed them getting up, so he discreetly checked them out as they left. He recognized one as Brett MacDonald, but he didn't know the other. Sawyer was several years younger than Brett, but he'd gone to school with Brett's little sister. She'd never liked Sawyer. The feeling was mutual.

"They said I can leave a stack of flyers here, too. Isn't it great?" Tess brushed his arm as she maneuvered around his chair to sit down again.

"It is," he said quietly. He couldn't get Brett's words off his mind. Did everyone think he was using Tess to get the ranch back?

Why wouldn't they think it? He'd been stupid to spend so much time in public with her. Hadn't considered how it would look.

"What's wrong?" She flashed him a concerned glance and took a drink of her coffee.

"Nothing." He attempted a smile and knew it fell flat. "I need to be getting back soon. I have a lot to do around the ranch now that Bud quit."

"Wait—Bud quit?"

"Yeah." He didn't realize Ken hadn't told her.

"I see." Her forehead wrinkled as she considered. "I wish I would have known. I could have been putting out the word for a part-time ranch hand."

Regret mingled with relief. At least they were on the same page in thinking Bud needed to be replaced.

"Your dad isn't hiring one."

"What?" she said loudly. Glancing around, she lowered her voice. "What do you mean?"

"He said he wasn't hiring anyone. That once he's better, he'll come out and help."

The vein in her neck pulsed.

"I'll talk to him," she said.

"It's okay. I'm handling it." He drained the final bit of his coffee as Tucker yawned.

"It's not okay. It's not. Especially after everything you've done for us."

"I didn't mean to upset you." He hadn't realized she'd feel so strongly about it.

"You didn't. My father did." She began shrugging her arms into her coat. "I won't take up any more of your time. We can head back now."

He didn't want to cause a scene, so he put on his jacket and zipped Tucker up, then followed her outside. In the crisp air, he set Tuck in the wagon and pulled the blanket over the boy.

The day couldn't end like this. "Tess, you weren't taking up my time. I…I enjoyed this. I liked spending the day with you."

"Yeah, well, I liked it, too." She averted her gaze and took a step forward.

Sawyer started pulling the wagon. "But?"

"But I don't like how my dad's treating you."

"He's looking out for the ranch. It's not personal."

"Just like my ex-husband looked out for his restaurants…" she muttered.

"What do you mean?"

"Nothing."

They passed several stores in silence. "Tess?"

"Yeah?"

"I overheard some guys talking. They think I'm putting the moves on you to get my hands on the ranch." Saying it out loud unearthed shame deep inside him. It was what Christina had done to him. He couldn't imagine doing that to someone else.

She barked out a laugh. "Really? Well, let them talk. I don't care what a couple of bored gossips say. I've heard worse."

He didn't respond. Wasn't sure how to. Both their reputations were on the line. His would never be clean. He didn't want hers soiled on account of him.

"I don't want—" he said.

"Rumors have spread about me since I moved back. I don't care what people say. The same people who said I'm a shrew who couldn't keep my husband happy are the ones yapping about us. The only person responsible for destroying my family is my ex-husband. Nothing I ever did was good enough for him. If they want to think otherwise, so be it." Her boots ate up the sidewalk quickly.

"Tess, wait." He grabbed her arm. She looked at him through glistening eyes. "I've had someone prey on me, use me. It was humiliating. I don't want you to ever think…"

She gave her head a small shake and looked at him like he'd just grown a third ear. "I would never think it, okay? Never."

Her faith in him humbled him. He wanted to be the man she seemed to think he was.

Ten minutes of sheer silence on the way home had done nothing to quiet the questions in her mind. Tucker's light snores from the back seat assured her he'd be out for the ride. At times, she'd wondered about Sawyer's dating history, but usually she shushed the thoughts.

What had he meant when he'd said someone preyed on him? Was it a woman? Or was it related to losing his inheritance?

She glanced his way. He looked tired. All day he'd been solid as a rock, helping with Tucker, silently supporting her as she'd gone to the businesses.

Who supported him? How had he gotten to be the man he was today? A good man, an honorable one, a guy a girl could lean on.

"Sawyer, what happened?" She couldn't hold it in another minute.

"What do you mean?" He glanced her way, then turned his attention back to the road.

"Back there. You mentioned someone preying on you. Was it a girl?"

His jaw shifted. She mentally chided herself. His past was none of her business.

But talking to him every afternoon, discussing the cattle and the weather and the extra equipment, bonding over the ranch and hanging out in town—well, she wanted it to be her business.

She'd grown close to him.

And since he clearly wasn't going to open up, she decided to go first.

"The ranch isn't mine, so it's stupid for anyone to say

you're trying to get it from me." She picked at a fingernail. "I know what it's like to be used, and you're not the type."

"How can you be so sure?"

"Because you actually listen to me. And look at all the sacrifices you're making. My ex used to get so mad at me when I told him the restaurants' expenses were so high. Wait—I take that back. He didn't get mad. He'd wave me off with a *yeah, yeah, yeah* and keep spending. It wasn't just high-end stuff for the restaurants. He took a big old salary. Bought whatever he wanted. Then the bills would come in. That's when he'd get mad. He'd yell at me like it was my fault. I put up with it. I shouldn't have. And now Tucker's getting the raw end of the deal."

"I'm sorry, Tess." His low voice comforted her. "I put up with stuff, too. Hindsight will keep you up at night."

"What did you put up with?"

The muscle in his cheek flickered.

"Never mind. It's obviously a sore subject." She stared out her window at the empty land speeding by and sighed.

"Her name was Christina." He kept his eyes straight ahead. "I've never told anyone about her, except Bridget. Bridget knows. I don't want anyone else to know."

"I won't tell anyone." She'd never been one to spill secrets. It only hurt those who had trusted her with them.

"I met her on spring break my senior year of high school. She was a force of nature. A bitty thing, determined to be a pop star. Had the voice to do it, too. She told me she was going to New York City after graduation and that I should come with. What can I say? My heart fell so hard my head never had a chance to catch up."

Tess's own heart sank hearing him speak. The pride and affection he'd had for this girl still came through.

"Dad didn't want me to. He asked—begged, really—for me to stay here and ranch with him. Up until Christina, I fully planned on it. Loved ranching. Loved working with him. But…"

"Like you said, your heart fell hard. I know." She'd had a similar experience with Devin. He'd been charming and funny and outgoing. Showered gifts on her. Taken her on expensive dates. Then after a short engagement, reality had set in.

"We figured we'd pool our resources. It's an expensive city. I thought nothing of it. I was mentally counting down the days to propose to her. I'd been there a month when Dad died. I couldn't think straight. It seemed impossible he could be gone. And Christina needed money for auditions, for her wardrobe, musicians, flights, demo tapes, you name it. Both our names were on the accounts."

She understood what he was saying. "She took it all, didn't she?"

His face was hard. He nodded.

"But it was so much money."

"You'd be surprised how quickly the cash runs out when you're trying to be a star."

"You broke it off when you found out?" The only missing piece was how it ended.

"Nope. I found out when I came home to an empty apartment. Bank account was drained dry. I had nothing. She moved in with her sleazeball agent."

"And her career?"

He shrugged. "Went nowhere, as far as I can tell."

"I'm sorry, Sawyer. That's awful. You didn't deserve that."

"I won't make that mistake again."

She wanted to ask what mistake—trusting a woman with his money? Trusting a woman at all? There were several she could think of right off the bat. But he'd already shared so much.

"Was there anything you could do? You know, legally?"

He met her eyes then, and sympathy flooded her at the pain in them.

"No. Like I said, her name was on my accounts." He shook his head. "I was a dumb kid. I've learned my lesson."

"It wasn't your fault."

"No use throwing the blame somewhere else."

"How about where it belongs? On her?"

"Look, Tess—" he glanced her way "—God's giving me a second chance here. You don't need a second chance unless you mess up the first one."

"Sometimes bad things happen to people through no fault of their own, though."

"If I don't learn from my mistakes, I'm bound to repeat them."

She slumped back in her seat. Had she learned from her mistakes? Was she bound to repeat them? She wasn't living only for herself anymore. She had Tucker to think about. And Sawyer made some good points.

Maybe she'd be wise to spend more time reading her Bible.

Chapter Nine

As a nineteen-year-old kid, Sawyer's pride had kept him from asking anyone for advice. As a grown man, he knew better than to let his pride overcome his need for counsel. Right now, he needed help.

He parked in the driveway next to the old two-story house nestled on Austin's ranch Tuesday evening. Making his way to the front door, he huddled in his jacket against the driving snow. He hadn't been here in years. Lights glowed from the windows, triggering memories he'd suppressed. How many times back in the day had he driven up to these same welcoming lights? A long-forgotten sensation of belonging came over him.

Before his feet hit the welcome mat, the door opened to Austin's grinning face. Within minutes, he'd ditched his outerwear and was sitting at the table with a bowl full of chili.

"It's good to have you here, man." Austin sat across from him, spoon poised near his mouth. "About time, too."

"I feel the same." Sawyer studied the space. A large living room opened to the dining area, and the kitchen was in the back. He remembered a bathroom and bedroom being on the main floor, with more bedrooms and another bathroom upstairs. A large mudroom stood off the kitchen. The place felt lived in, a little messy, comfortable. "I like what you've done."

Austin swallowed his bite and shrugged. "Wasn't much. Some paint, new floors. Got rid of those ugly chandeliers. The kitchen could use remodeling, but I don't want to deal with it. Too much of a hassle."

He nodded, reaching for a piece of corn bread. "I'm looking forward to the day I own a house."

"Are you looking?"

"No. I need to save up for a down payment first. This ranch, the house—it fits you."

"It does fit. After Dad died, it didn't for a while. Mostly because I expected Randy to want what I wanted." Austin stared up at the corner of the ceiling for a moment with a thoughtful expression. "He'd just graduated. About the same age as you were when your dad passed. I was hard on him. We worked it out."

"He still lives here, right?"

"Yeah, but he's always going on about getting a place near town to be close to the shop. All talk, of course."

"Does he help with the ranch at all?"

"Nope. Ranching's not his thing. I still don't see how my own brother can like fishing more than cattle. He and Dad and I worked this ranch together our entire lives. When he told me he was opening the store, I about blew a gasket. He's done well for himself, though. Watkins' Outfitters is thriving. Going on eight years now. Eight. Can you believe it? The time sure goes by quick."

"You work the ranch alone?"

"No, oh, no." He shook his head as if the thought was

ludicrous. "I hired Bo Nichol full-time before Randy quit on me. I have a few part-timers on the payroll, too. One's in high school. Another works a few days a week year-round for me."

"On a ranch the size of Ken's, how many ranch hands would be ideal?" He continued eating, watching Austin carefully for his reaction.

"It's about the same size as mine, a little smaller, not much. I'd say it needs someone managing it full-time and one full-time cowboy. Two part-time hands to pick up the slack."

"So two full-timers and some part-time help."

"Yeah. Why? Are you looking to hire someone? I can help with that if need be. Say the word and I'll get you a list of people who might be interested. I heard Bud Delta quit."

"He did. Ken isn't replacing him." He wouldn't bad-mouth his employer or former employee, but if he was going to ask for advice, Austin needed to know what was going on.

"What?" Austin blinked and stared at him.

Sawyer sighed. "Ken thinks he'll feel good enough to help soon."

Austin's spoon plinked against the table. "Is he trying to hasten his death? No, don't answer that. I was being sarcastic."

Sawyer chewed a bite of corn bread.

"Let me get this straight. You're running the McKay ranch solo? All of it. Just you."

"Well, Tess takes care of the finances."

"Okay, so you don't deal with the books. But the feeding, checking, repairing—all the rest? You. Only you?"

"As of Saturday, yes."

"That's messed up." Austin picked up his spoon again and took another bite.

"I know. What I don't know is what to do about it."

"Have you talked to him?"

"I have."

"Stubborn," he muttered. Then he tapped his chin. "You have three choices. Kill yourself running it alone, hire another ranch hand or quit."

His thoughts exactly. "I don't like any of the options. It's tough doing it by myself. Ken won't let me hire anyone. And if I quit, the cattle suffer." As well as Tess. And Tucker.

"I hear you."

They both sat for a moment with their thoughts.

"You can always work for me." Compassion gleamed in Austin's eyes.

"Nah, I'll be fine." He believed in earning his keep. Austin didn't need another ranch hand. "I've been praying, and I guess I wanted your take on the situation."

"You don't owe them anything, Sawyer." The words were honest.

Logically, Austin was correct. Sawyer didn't owe Ken anything. He was a worker for hire. An employee. But he understood why Ken didn't want to hire anyone else. He couldn't afford to.

But Sawyer wasn't staying on out of duty to Ken.

"You grew up on the ranch," Austin said. "You want it to succeed. Guys like us can't help it. The land means something to us. But…"

"It does mean something. I wish it would have meant the same to me after Dad died. I could have used some tough talk then." Would he have listened, though? His head and heart had been so wrapped up in Christina, nothing would have changed his mind about selling the ranch.

"Why'd you do it?" Austin leveled a stare his way. "Why didn't you hold on to it? Was it too tough thinking of ranching without your dad around?"

How he wished he could answer in the affirmative. His skin itched as a battle launched inside his mind. This was Austin. His best friend. The guy who had never given up on him, and who probably never would. Couldn't he trust him with the truth?

Austin deserved to know.

"No, that wasn't it." He clenched his jaw, willing the words to come. *God, if I can't be honest with Austin, I'll never be the man I want to be. I have to tell him.*

Austin raised his hands in defense. "I've never asked. You never told me. If you need to keep the reason with you to the grave, I respect that. It won't change anything between us."

"I want to tell you." Sawyer's gaze locked with his. "You've never given up on me." He started to get choked up. Cleared his throat. "It was Christina."

"I figured as much."

Up until Dad died, Sawyer had talked to Austin all the time, telling him about Christina and their plans. After the funeral, he'd shut down. Cut himself off from everyone back home.

"I didn't spend the inheritance or gamble it away like the town thinks."

"I know." Austin crossed his arms over his chest and leaned back. "I know you better than to think that."

"And it wasn't drugs or anything, either. It's easier letting people believe what they want. The truth is Christina wanted to be a star. I wanted to help. I didn't see any harm in having joint accounts. I was ready to marry her."

"She stole it?" He sounded incredulous. Sawyer wasn't sure what to believe. He didn't think Christina set out to take all his money, but having it at her fingertips made her feel like it was hers. And soon, she'd made sure it was.

"I wouldn't say stole, exactly. Making it in the music industry isn't cheap. I was fine with bankrolling her expenses. We had a joint bank account, and after she landed an agent, she dumped me. The account was empty. Didn't even say goodbye."

Austin stood, rubbing the back of his neck, and began pacing.

"Did you get a lawyer? Sue her? I can't believe she did that to you."

He'd been bracing himself for *how could you be so stupid?* He should have known Austin would support him. "It was my fault. I should have protected my money better. I was in love with her. Infatuated. No one could have talked sense into me. I wouldn't have listened. She was all that mattered."

Austin's lips flashed into a self-deprecating smile. "We were hotheads, weren't we? I knew everything when I graduated high school, or so I thought. I'm sorry she did that to you, man."

"Thanks."

"Don't worry. I'll never tell anyone what really happened with your inheritance."

"I know. You're a man of honor. You keep your word." He wished he'd trusted him with all this sooner.

"I try. Don't always succeed. Wish I could be of more help in your current situation, though."

"Thanks for never giving up on me."

"Never would. I missed you, Sawyer. I miss having you around. It wasn't until you'd moved away that I understood how much I'd lost with you gone. You're irreplaceable."

"Hardly. I barely talked to you for over a decade." Regrets overwhelmed him. He'd missed out on so much.

"I hounded you until you did." Austin grinned. "You were the one who pulled my car out of the ditch after I snuck to Jana's house against Dad's orders. You were the one who told me to do my homework in eighth grade or I'd lose respect for myself and become a loser. You forced me to lift weights all of sophomore year when I got cut from the basketball team. I thank God I have you for a friend. Who knows where I'd be if you hadn't been around, kicking my behind?"

"I didn't come home for your dad's funeral." Sawyer's eyes stung with tears of shame. "Can you ever forgive me for that?"

"No need to." His chin rose. "I did years ago."

"Look, I've made a mess of my life." He hadn't told Austin about working for half pay. It wouldn't be fair to Tess or Ken for him to discuss the ranch's finances. Would Austin feel differently about him if he knew the financial sacrifice he was already making? "Sometimes I feel like I'm destined to repeat my past mistakes."

"I know what you mean. But see the Christmas tree?" Austin pointed to the tall spruce twinkling with white lights. Sawyer nodded. "It's a reminder of God's grace. Unearned. Look to it whenever you get down on yourself and it will help you look up. God gives us all the strength we need."

Unearned grace. Instead of looking down on himself, he should raise his eyes to God's love. Exactly what he'd needed to hear.

Tess drew her favorite blanket over her lap as she watched a Christmas baking show in her room that evening. Tucker was sleeping down the hall, and Daddy had turned in early. Usually she watched television in the living room after supper, but she was hoping Devin would return her call and she didn't want Daddy to overhear her. Earlier, she'd left another message with her ex to call her when he got out of work.

The closer it got to Christmas, the more she wanted to make sure Tucker had some time with his father. Last year, she'd been so angry she hadn't cared when he canceled coming to Sunrise Bend at the last minute. He'd planned on spending two days with Tucker, but then claimed he got the flu. He hadn't rescheduled. His parents had mailed a few gifts to Tucker, though. None from him.

Devin hadn't even made plans to come here for Tucker's birthday. She'd offered to bring Tuck there but had been met with lame excuses. As usual.

Did he even think of Tucker as his child anymore? Or did he only have room in his heart for Riley?

Checking her phone again, she scowled. No messages. Reaching across the bed to her nightstand, she grabbed the Bible. It had been her mother's, and before that, her grandmother's. Paging through it, she had no idea what she was looking for. Wasn't looking for anything, really, just a passage to take her mind off the fact so many things had gone wrong in her life.

Her husband had left her for another woman. Through no fault of his own, Tucker lacked a father. The ranch wasn't profitable. Daddy's cancer was still there—although the last treatment may have halted the spread.

And in addition to all of the above, she couldn't stop thinking about Sawyer.

Was that why she was pushing so hard for Devin to spend time with Tucker? Out of guilt?

Maybe Devin's lack of interest in their son was her fault. If she had tried harder at their marriage, maybe he wouldn't have strayed. If she hadn't been so angry about him cheating on her and getting Tiffany pregnant while she—his wife—was pregnant, maybe she wouldn't have let him cancel all his visitations.

The Bible fell open at the book of Romans. *And not only so, but we glory in tribulations also: knowing that tribulation worketh patience; And patience, experience; and experience, hope.*

Tribulations, patience, experience, hope. She closed the Bible. Patience had never been her strong suit. But… She looked back over the past months. Daddy's cancer was a tribulation, but it had also given her a chance to care for him, to be here with him every day, which in her mind was a blessing. Then there was Devin's lack of interest in their son—another tribulation—but so far all that had accomplished was to wear her down.

Maybe tribulations *did* work patience. She'd certainly gained experience through the bad stuff.

What about the last part, though, the hope?

Tribulations, patience, experience, hope.

Until Sawyer had arrived, her hope had been almost snuffed out. Spending time with him every afternoon had changed her. She anticipated seeing him. Tucker did, too. Sawyer played with her son, listened to her and cared about the ranch. He had great ideas—ones she never would have come up with—and sometimes he looked at her with a gleam in his eye that made her blush.

She'd been thinking of that gleam too often lately. Wondering if he ever thought about pulling her into his arms and kissing her the way she kept thinking about him.

Her phone rang, and she jumped, clapping her palm on her chest. Pushing the Bible aside, she answered it.

"I have to make this quick," Devin said.

Annoyance flared. He always had to make it quick. She rarely contacted him. Did he really think she wanted so much of his precious time?

"Christmas is right around the corner." She tried not to sound naggy and harsh, but she failed. Nothing new. "When are you going to see Tucker?"

"I don't know." He sighed. "It's busy here. You know how it is. Christmas parties and…"

"He's your son, Devin." She wouldn't let him weasel out of this.

"I know, and I miss him." *Liar.* A muffled kid's cry came through the line. Was Devin watching Riley? "I just got off work, and…"

"And you're with your other child." Why did it make her so angry that he was with Riley? She forced herself not to explode. "I realize having kids six months apart isn't ideal, but you can't pretend one doesn't exist."

"I don't. I never…" he blustered. "You're the one who moved away."

"You stopped showing up for your weekends long before I moved back."

"Yeah, well, it's busy, and I…"

She waited to hear his latest explanation. None came. "I'll make it easy on you," she said. "I'll drive to Laramie Saturday. You can see Tucker before work." He never went into the restaurant before four o'clock. "If your parents want to see him, I'll stop by their house that night."

A long silence stretched.

"Okay." He sounded like a condemned man.

"And, Devin?" Her chest got a fluttery, sinking feeling. It had to be said, and it hurt her to have to say this. "Make sure Tuck has a Christmas present from you."

"Fine." The crying in the background grew to epic levels. "I've got to go. Riley needs me. See you on Saturday." And the line went dead.

The emotions she'd been bottling up, trying to ignore, pretending didn't exist, all erupted out of her.

She sat there blinking repeatedly with the phone in her hand.

How dare he?

How dare he claim Riley needed him? Didn't he get it? Tucker needed him, too. He acted as if their son didn't matter. As if his life with her had never happened.

Her throat swelled. She couldn't draw a full breath. All she knew was she had to get out of this stifling room, get some fresh air before the hurt squeezed all the oxygen from her lungs. She quietly made her way downstairs, slid her feet into boots, put her jacket on and wound a scarf around her neck. Then she slipped out the side door and walked toward the stables with her hands jammed into her coat pockets.

Under the half-moon and black sky, tears dropped onto her cheeks, and she wiped them away, furious with herself for crying. For caring.

It hurt. Knowing Devin was taking care of his other child—likely seeing her every day—and couldn't be bothered to celebrate his son's birthday or Christmas was like a knife to the gut. What had Tucker ever done to him? If Devin wanted to be mad at her, fine, but he shouldn't be taking it out on his son.

A hiccup escaped as headlights flashed from behind. She got out of the way, jogging to stand under the stable door so Sawyer's truck could pass, but it slowed. The wreath above her made a scratching sound against the wood as a breeze rustled through. He rolled down his window. "What are you doing out here?"

"Nothing." Her voice was high and squeaky. "Just taking a walk."

He glanced away and met her gaze again. "At nine thirty?"

"Yep. Good time to stretch the legs." Her voice cracked at the end, and she fought tears back as best she could, but they began to flow steadily down her cheeks again.

He turned off the engine and got out of the truck.

As his long legs strode toward her, her mortification grew. She couldn't stop crying. Wished she could suddenly turn invisible. Wished he would go away and let her wallow in her misery.

Wished Sawyer would wrap her in his arms.

And that was just what he did.

He shouldn't have gotten out of the truck. And he definitely shouldn't have pulled her into his arms and let her sob against his chest.

But he had. And at the moment, he had no regrets. They could wait until later.

He didn't say a word, just rubbed her back and let her cry it out. The reason for her tears was the mystery. Was it Ken? Had he gotten bad news about his health? Or had she had a tough day with Tucker? Being a single mom wasn't easy. As her chest heaved in an attempt to get her emotions under control, something inside him grew strong, full of resolve.

Whatever had made her cry, he would do anything to fix it.

He caressed her hair, unnerved at how silky it felt through his fingers, and when she shivered, he tipped her chin up to look at him.

He planned on asking her what was wrong.

But his plan fell apart at the sight of her big brown eyes full of tears. They shimmered, implored him to not think less of her for crying, as if he could.

The words he wanted to say, the questions he wanted to ask vanished as quickly as the faint trail of their breaths in the cold air. His hands moved down to her lower back, and his gaze fell to her lips.

"I want to kiss you," he said, his face close to hers.

Her pupils grew big and dark, and she softly nodded. "Then kiss me."

He didn't need to be asked twice.

The instant his mouth met hers, he pressed her closer to him. He'd waited a long time—too long—to kiss a woman. And Tess wasn't just any woman. He tasted the salt of her tears and wanted to fix everything wrong in her life. Then she was kissing him back and all thoughts vanished. Her mouth opened to let him explore, and he did, slowly, gently.

He'd give about anything to her, for her, right this minute.

Fighting himself to end the kiss when all he really wanted was to make it last, he finally broke away.

She rocked back, her eyes glistening. "I wasn't expecting that."

"Neither was I." He let go of her and raked his hand through his hair. "I don't know if I should apologize or…"

"Why? Was it bad for you?"

"No, it wasn't bad. Are you kidding? It was great. Better than great." His hands couldn't seem to stay away from her, so he settled them against her lower back again. "Amazing."

"Yes. Amazing." She hugged him then, and he inhaled her flowery shampoo.

"What has you so upset?"

Her face fell. "My ex."

"Oh." He wasn't sure what to say. "Anything I can help with?"

"I've been trying to get him to see Tucker for Christmas, and he's full of excuses. I finally talked to him tonight. I'm driving there on Saturday, basically forcing him to see Tucker. I told you he has a daughter, right? Riley's six months younger than Tuck." She pressed her lips together and stared up at the starry sky a moment. "She was crying in the background."

He still didn't know what to say, so he kept quiet.

"He told me he had to go because Riley needed him. *Riley* needed him. Like Tuck doesn't?" She shivered. "I hate that my son basically doesn't have a dad. And I hate that I'm jealous of my ex's little girl. His daughter didn't do anything. But I resent her—a child, practically a baby—I resent her so much, Sawyer. I feel like a monster."

He tugged her close to him. "You're not a monster. It's normal."

"It's not normal. My life isn't normal. And I want Tucker to have normal, you know? A daddy who cares about him, even if we're not together. But Tucker doesn't get that. Riley does. It's not fair, and I can't change it, and I hate it. I hate it."

He stroked her hair. "I hate it, too."

Anger made his muscles tense. What man neglected his own son? What kind of guy did that? And to leave Tess and Tucker vulnerable while her dad was so ill— it was wrong. If her ex were here, Sawyer would have a few choice words to say to him.

He held her gently until her trembling stopped. Finally, she sighed and stepped out of his embrace.

"Well, now you know how awful I am." She looked everywhere but at him.

"You're not awful. You're good. A good mother. A good daughter. A good friend."

"Are we friends?" she asked softly.

"You know we are."

"We've both been hurt."

"Yes."

"I don't want to hurt you."

Did she plan on hurting him? He frowned. "Then don't."

"I won't." She nodded, staring up into his eyes. "If we're going to be friends, we can never kiss again. It's too confusing otherwise."

Never kiss again? He shifted his jaw.

Even if they never kissed again, he'd be reliving this one for years to come. Looking into her pretty brown eyes, his stomach sank.

He'd fallen in love with Tess Malone.

It was too late to protect his heart.

"Fine." He growled. "We never kiss again."

He was terrible at love anyway. She was doing him a favor. It felt like a big fat rejection, though.

Maybe this was a sign. Ken had changed the rules of his employment. And Tess was setting the rules of their relationship. He seemed to have no say in the matter.

He wasn't making any money working here. And now Tess demanded he stay in the friend zone.

He'd given both of them too much. He didn't know how much longer he'd be willing to sacrifice for people who didn't appreciate him.

Chapter Ten

Two hours into the visit with Devin on Saturday afternoon, Tess's head began to throb. All week she'd been trying to get her mind off Sawyer's kiss. She'd spent four hours on the drive here thinking about him. How she'd been avoiding him since Tuesday, how she wished she were spending the day with him in Sunrise Bend rather than in Laramie basically forcing Devin to acknowledge his son.

She wasn't a fool—Devin loved Riley more than Tucker. Why wouldn't he? He was with the girl all the time. But that didn't mean he could pretend his boy didn't exist.

Looking around for the fifteenth time since arriving, she tried to reconcile what she'd thought to be true with the actual truth. Clearly, Tiffany and Riley lived here. Tess hadn't realized they'd moved in after she and Tucker moved out. Thankfully, Tiffany wasn't here today.

The two still hadn't set a wedding date, either. Strange, since Devin had been in such a hurry to divorce Tess to start his new life with Tiffany. Yet they hadn't gotten around to getting married. Odd.

The house hadn't changed. Same furniture, same

paintings on the wall. The play kitchen, dolls and stuffed animals were new. But the dining table, couch and chairs, even the lamps were the same. White garland and colorful Christmas lights were strung haphazardly on the fireplace mantel.

Riley toddled over to Devin with her arms raised for him to pick her up.

"Show Tucker your kitty, Riley." Devin pointed to the corner full of toys. The first time he'd instructed Riley to show Tucker something, poison had shot through Tess's heart. She'd been convinced he was showing off his little girl.

But about an hour ago, she'd realized the truth. Every time the girl wanted attention from him, he shooed her away.

He couldn't be bothered to actually play with his own kids. And that included Riley.

Tucker had no idea who he was. He didn't recognize him as his daddy. In fact, he'd hung back with Tess for the first twenty minutes. Devin had made no effort with him, either. The man was positively awkward with both children.

Tucker handed Riley a stuffed cat, and she hugged it tightly before giggling and handing it to him.

They were cute together. Really cute. Her heart warmed at the sight.

"Look, I hate to wrap this up, but I've got to get ready for work." With a look of panic, he pushed up from the chair. "I got him a gift. It's at Ma and Pop's. You're still going over there, right?"

That was code for his mom bought Tucker a gift. The man couldn't even take a lousy trip to the store to buy Tucker a Christmas present. Why had she married him?

She propped on a smile. "Yes, I am."

"Okay, good." He jerked his thumb to the staircase. "Mind if I get ready?"

She glared at him, her mouth agape. Was he really suggesting she watch his daughter while he dressed for work? The nerve!

"Right." He had the grace to look embarrassed. "I'll, ah, get ready after you leave."

A sense of pity washed over her. His hair was receding, he'd gained a good fifteen pounds since the divorce and the bags under his eyes sagged. He seemed edgy and impatient. Like it was too hard for him to put on his fake act much longer.

She knew that act well. And she was glad to not have to deal with it anymore.

"You know what? Why don't you go ahead and get ready." A burst of charity filled her. "I'll watch the kids, and when you're done, I'll take off."

"You don't mind?" He sounded confused.

"I don't." She glanced at the play area where Tucker and Riley were exchanging stuffed animals. "They're siblings. And they seem to like each other."

He stared at the kids for a long moment, and the corner of his mouth curved up. "Yeah, they do."

As he jogged up the staircase, Tess was draped with a sense of peace. She'd come here with a chip on her shoulder. She'd had something to prove—mainly that Tucker had as much right to Devin as Riley did. But her resentment toward the little girl with the dark curls and shy smile had completely disappeared.

Tess saw Devin for what he was. A selfish man not up to accepting his responsibilities.

She'd drive over to his parents' house in a little bit,

and maybe they would fuss over Tucker, maybe they wouldn't, but she'd rest easy knowing she'd tried. And afterward, she and Tuck would snuggle together in the hotel room she'd booked. Tomorrow morning they'd have pancakes at her favorite diner in Laramie. Then they'd drive back to Sunrise Bend.

Back home, where they were loved.

Riley brought a book over to Tess and set it on her lap. The girl looked up at her with impossibly big brown eyes. Tucker ran up, too. "Read, Mama." He jabbed at the book, and Riley smiled.

"Okay. Come on up here, you two." She lifted Riley and set her on the couch to her left as Tucker scrambled up and sat to her right. She opened the sensory book, which had a mama bunny and baby bunny on the cover, and enjoyed the warm cuddliness of two toddlers pressed against her. She proceeded to read the story, pausing for them to pet the bunny ears and feel the scratch of the bunny's tongue.

Lord, thank You for bringing me here. Thank You for showing me the truth about Devin. I'm glad I could meet his little girl. And forgive me for resenting her. Watch over her. She needs You, too.

Devin's heavy footsteps on the staircase made her close the book. She kissed the top of Riley's head, then Tucker's, and announced it was time to go.

"It was nice to meet you, Riley." She bent to hug the child. "We'll see you again."

Devin picked up Tucker. "You be good for your mother now, okay?"

He nodded.

He set him back down and met her eyes. "Thanks, Tess, for bringing him today."

She nodded, took Tucker by the hand and left.

She'd thought Devin needed to see his son. But it turned out she was the one who'd needed the visit. In time, they might be able to have a better relationship for Tucker's sake. She'd do her part. Hopefully, Devin would do his, too.

He'd been in a bad mood all day. Sawyer finished checking the cattle Saturday morning and headed to the ranch office. He'd seen Tess drive away earlier and had said a little prayer for her visit with her ex to go well. He hadn't spoken to her much since Tuesday night.

Ken had been coming out every afternoon in her place. He'd putter around the pole barn, complaining about not being able to find the parts he'd ordered months ago. Sawyer calmly directed him to the storage room, where everything was organized on shelves. Or he would saddle up one of the horses and ride out, coming back within twenty minutes to badger Sawyer about a section of fence that was down. But Sawyer had checked the fence, and it wasn't down.

With Ken being such a pain, Sawyer couldn't help wishing Tess were the one checking in with him like before.

He missed her.

He never should have kissed her.

She wanted to be friends. Just friends.

And he supposed he should be grateful for her honesty. He was a ranch employee. A friend. Not a boyfriend.

He was still trying to figure out how to have a future here. Still trying to be a man his father would be proud of. Which was why, regardless of how Tess felt about him, he was keeping his promise to her to cut costs and increase profits. At least through January. After that, he was asking for his full pay. If they didn't want to give it to him, he would quit.

The office door was open and the light was on. Ken must have come out a little early. Sawyer slowed, taking off his gloves. Ken sat behind the desk, looked up and waved him in.

"Good, you're here. We need to talk." Ken wore a Carhartt jacket and black stocking cap. He set down his pen, rested his hands on his stomach and leaned back in the chair. The set of his jaw made the hair on the back of Sawyer's neck bristle. He'd seen that look before, and it didn't bode well. "Now that I'm done with chemo, it's high time I took charge of this place again."

What did he mean *take charge of this place*? "When you hired me, you said you were retiring."

Ken's eyes flashed with guilt as he looked away. "Things change."

"What things?" Sawyer asked.

"Since Tess blabbed to you about the finances, you know what's at stake. I'll be managing everything from now on."

Ken was managing everything? How would that work?

"What will I do?"

"What you're doing now." He drummed his fingertips against the desk. "Feeding, checking and working the cattle. Chores."

So if he was doing exactly what he was doing now, what was Ken proposing?

"You'll be part-time, though," Ken said. "No need for two people doing a job one can do."

Disbelief crashed over him, followed by an incredulous hurt. This was how he was being repaid for his sacrifices? By being demoted?

Wanting to shout at the man, he forced himself to remain calm. "How exactly will I be able to do all the chores I'm doing now if I'm only here part-time?"

"You won't waste it shuffling my stuff around, that's for sure." His face reddened. "Spend your time where it counts. On the cattle."

"What do you think I've been doing?" The words squeezed out of his throat. "I've been devoting all my time to this place. If it storms, I ride out in the middle of the night to check on any vulnerable cows. In the wee hours of the morning, I feed the cattle, and then I take the time to keep track of how much they actually eat. I pore over feeding systems, hay production and any trace minerals the cows might need. I've inventoried your equipment, done routine maintenance on your tractors, cleaned this place up well past working hours. During my free time, I've even replaced shingles on some of the outbuildings. You think I can do all that part-time?" His voice rose. "I can't even do it full-time."

"It's what you're paid to do." Ken's chin tilted high.

"No, it isn't, and you know that, too. I'm barely getting paid as it is. I'm certainly not earning enough to do everything I just listed."

"You agreed to my terms." Ken glared at him. "Starting today, you'll be paid by the hour. And you'll owe me rent come January first."

Part-time pay. And now rent.

"I don't think so, Ken." He stood. All the questions in his mind had been answered. He had no doubt what he was supposed to do. "If you think this ranch can be run by one person, and you're dead set on managing it, it's all yours. I quit."

"You can't quit." He sprang to his feet, almost tipping the chair over. "You need this job."

"No, I don't." Sawyer pivoted to leave. "I'll pack the cabin and be gone before sundown."

Silence was the only response.

He let himself out, looking straight ahead to numb himself from the pain. It had begun to snow, and he let out a shaky exhalation. He noted things as he walked past. The stables were tidy, the corrals neat. The ranch was in much better shape now than when he'd arrived last month.

He thought of his father. His life here as a kid—just the two of them. And a sense of rightness permeated him.

Dad, you'd be proud of me right now. I cleaned this place up. Got it running efficiently. And I didn't cave to Ken's pressure. I'm worth more than what he thinks. I'm living life on my terms now.

His cabin came into view, the Christmas tree visible from the window.

Austin had said it was a reminder to look up at God's grace instead of looking down with regrets.

No regrets. He'd done the right thing. God would take care of him. He knew it.

Taking the porch steps two at a time, he paused before his front door.

He'd miss Tess. Miss Tucker.

But she only wanted to be friends, and he wanted so much more.

It was better all around that he left now. Before his fickle heart wavered and agreed to be Ken's servant just to make life easier for Tess and her son.

He'd done that for a woman once.

He'd never do it again.

Tess sipped herbal tea in front of Devin's parents' Christmas tree after having supper with them later that night. Margaret and Daniel Malone had been doting on Tucker since the minute she'd carried him inside. Their affection for him had caught her off guard. This visit was nothing like she'd expected. She'd figured her ex in-laws would be standoffish with her and formal with Tucker. She'd assumed they reserved all their love for little Riley.

But Tess had been wrong. They'd been warm and welcoming—embracing her with joyful tears earlier. They'd fussed over Tucker, let him pet their old basset hound, Penny, and showered him with affection. Daniel had helped him make worms out of Play-Doh, and Margaret had guided him through a few pages of a Christmas-themed sticker book.

Now the two of them were helping him unwrap gifts and clapping their hands as soon as a present emerged.

Tess set her mug on a coaster and took out her phone to snap a few pictures. Once she'd gotten them, she reclined back with questions tumbling around her head.

Daniel and Margaret hadn't seen Tucker in well over a year, and she'd assumed it was because they liked Tiffany better than her and had Riley to spoil. However, they were genuinely enjoying their grandson, and they'd been gracious to her all evening. Which meant she'd been wrong about them.

Then why had Devin and his family cut Tucker out of their lives?

She wouldn't ruin a nice evening with questions she

didn't really need to know the answers to. What was done was done.

"You didn't need to do all this." Tess gestured to the toys and books piled next to Tuck.

A shadow dimmed Daniel's expression. "It's not nearly enough."

What a strange thing to say.

Tucker plunked down on Daniel's lap and twisted to look up at him, showing him the stuffed horse in his hands. Margaret crossed over and sat next to Tess on the couch.

"It was very kind, very generous of you to drive all this way to let us see Tucker." Margaret squeezed Tess's hand. Pain flitted through her eyes, though she smiled. "We had so much fun shopping for him."

"You're his grandparents. You're family. I wouldn't deprive him of that."

Margaret exchanged a glance with Daniel.

He carried Tucker over and set him on Margaret's lap. She kissed his temple and held him close as he pretended to make the horse trot through the air. Then he let out a big yawn and snuggled into her chest.

Tess watched them with affection. It had been a busy day for the little guy. No wonder he was tired.

Daniel took a seat across from them. "We did you a disservice, Tess, and I speak for both of us when I say we're sorry."

"We didn't do right by you." Margaret's eyes glistened with tears.

What were they talking about? Yes, the entire family had dropped her and Tucker like old worn-out shoes once the divorce was final, but she didn't really blame

Daniel and Margaret. Devin had put them in an awkward situation.

"You have nothing to apologize for." Tess shook her head. "Devin and I couldn't make our marriage work. It had nothing to do with you."

"But the divorce..." Margaret's lips pinched together. "We didn't realize you'd be left with so little."

Understanding dawned. The restaurants. Of course. But she hadn't expected to get anything from them anyhow. "I didn't want anything from the restaurants. They're yours. Don't worry about it another minute."

Margaret glued her attention to the top of Tucker's head.

"When Devin told us about you two splitting up, he made it sound like he could lose everything." Daniel's eyes implored her. "But once the divorce was final..." He scowled, shaking his head.

"What he's trying to say is we saw the truth. Tiffany moved into your house within the week. They went on a fancy cruise. All of your furniture was still there. You didn't take any of it."

"I didn't want or need it. Daddy has a house full of furniture."

They exchanged another glance.

"You were left with so little in the divorce," Daniel said. "What, a few thousand dollars? Well, that and the monthly child support from our son."

"Yeah, that sums it up." Where were they going with this? She hadn't expected to get rich off the divorce. She and Devin had lived paycheck to paycheck their entire marriage.

"Devin has a sizable inheritance coming from us."

The inheritance wasn't a surprise. She didn't know

how much it would be and didn't care. She wasn't part of their lives anymore. They could do what they wanted with their money. It had nothing to do with her.

"It doesn't matter to me. He's your son."

"When you and Devin were married, he misled us about a few things," Daniel said. "He regularly asked for extra money. He insinuated you were a spendthrift. We didn't mind helping you kids out, but when he told us about the divorce, we made sure he had a good lawyer. We thought you were going to try to get money from the restaurants. We were wrong."

Tess stilled as the impact of his statement hit her. They'd thought *she* was the one with the spending problem?

"By keeping everything in our name, we shortchanged you. Devin still has the income from the restaurants, the house, the furniture and an inheritance to fall back on. But you? The divorce left you without much." Margaret's shoulders slumped in regret.

Tess didn't see it that way. She had her son. She had the privilege of taking care of Daddy. And she had finally gotten some freedom. "I've never needed a lot of money. But one thing the divorce did take was you two. I want Tucker to have grandparents, you know?"

Daniel stood, crossed over to the mantel and took an envelope from behind a glass reindeer. "We want you to have this. We should have given it to you after the divorce, but we didn't."

She held up her hands, palms out. "I don't want anything from you."

"Please, Tess, take it." Margaret's eyes pleaded. "We want you to have it."

"No. Not necessary. Devin and I fought all the time

about money. Our finances were our own fault." She didn't want to know what was in the envelope. She wouldn't take it. "When we were married, you two gave me something better than money. You gave me your love. You made me part of the family. I hope you'll give Tucker the same."

Before they could respond, she had to find out the one thing that still bothered her. "Why did you stop wanting to see Tucker? I know Devin drove him over here on his weekends with our original visitation schedule."

"We loved taking care of our little Tuck." Margaret beamed. "We would have gladly taken a lifetime of weekends with him."

"Our son didn't give us a choice." Daniel frowned. "After Tiffany gave birth to Riley, things changed."

She could guess what had happened. Tiffany didn't want them spending time with Tucker when they could be spending it with their new granddaughter.

Margaret sighed. "We didn't know you were moving back in with your dad or that Devin had stopped visiting Tucker altogether. And we were too embarrassed to speak to you privately."

"I wish you would have," Tess said. "I really hate that Tucker is missing out on an entire side of his family."

"Take this." Daniel held the envelope out to her again.

"No, I truly don't want it." She shook her head, feeling lighter. "The best gift you can give me is to spend time with your grandson. If you care to visit, give me a call. And I'll bring him down here now and then. He and Riley hit it off."

"I would have loved to have seen it. Precious babies." A tear fell on Margaret's cheek. She wiped it away. "Thank you."

"We don't deserve your kindness, but we sure appreciate it." Daniel's voice was gruff with emotion. He came over, and she stood as he wrapped her into a hug.

"I can say the same about you. Thanks for spending those weekends with Tucker. I know you loved on him. And I'm glad we could clear the air today. I honestly had no idea the divorce settlement bothered you. Like I said, it's not important to me." She hugged him and turned to Margaret. "I hate to break up the party, but it's time I got this little fella to bed."

Margaret handed Tucker to her. "Thank you. Thanks for letting us be part of his life."

"I always wanted you to be." She looked in Margaret's weepy, grateful eyes and got choked up herself.

"I'll load the car while you bundle up our grandson." Daniel began piling the gifts in his arms.

Ten minutes later, she waved goodbye to them. Daniel had his arm slung over Margaret's shoulders on the other side of the glass storm door as they waved.

Her head swam with revelations as she backed out of their driveway and pulled onto the road to head to the hotel. Her conclusions had been wrong. She'd thought having Riley around was the reason Devin and his parents cut Tucker out of their lives. But it was their own guilt.

How could his parents not have known she wanted them to see Tucker no matter what?

She had the strongest urge to call Sawyer. To tell him what had happened. Here, she'd been holding a grudge against a small child for supposedly turning Devin's family against her son when guilt and miscommunication were the real culprits.

Forgive me, Lord, for thinking the worst about them.

Help me keep a pure heart when it comes to Riley and Margaret and Daniel. When envy creeps in, remind me of Your grace tonight.

At the stoplight, she turned left and noted the Christmas lights strung around the trees through town. She was glad she had come. Thankful she'd made the effort. Grateful to clear the air. Who knew how many years could have passed with Tuck not spending time with Devin and his family? Their relationship left a lot to be desired, but at least they'd jump-started it again.

She wasn't naive enough to think they'd all spend lots of time together or that Devin would suddenly be the father Tucker needed, but it was okay.

Tucker already had men in his life who enjoyed spending time with him. Sawyer had paid more attention to Tucker in the past month than Devin had his entire life. And Daddy savored the moments he could spend with his grandson.

The hotel's parking lot entrance was up ahead. She turned into it and found a spot.

If Devin had been honest with her and his parents, this situation could have been avoided. If Daniel and Margaret had reached out to her after the divorce, she would have brought Tucker to see them. But none of them had been brave enough to have the conversation.

Honesty, transparency—they were vital in a relationship.

She hadn't been honest or transparent with Sawyer, and he was a thousand times the man Devin could ever hope to be. Sawyer had treated her with respect since the day they'd met. He treated her like an equal, listened to her opinions, asked for her advice. And he stepped up and did the hard stuff no one else wanted to do.

Why was she fighting her feelings for him?

Hadn't she known since his kiss she'd fallen in love with the man?

She'd fallen in love with him and had no idea what to do about it.

Maybe the long drive home tomorrow would give her some insight. For now, she wanted nothing more than to carry her sweet boy into the hotel room, crawl under the covers and sleep through the night. She'd had enough for one day. Everything else would have to wait.

Chapter Eleven

"Thanks again, man, for letting me crash here." Sawyer helped check cattle on Austin's ranch the next morning. It had been a long night, but he didn't mind getting up at the crack of dawn to come out here and do what he loved. The mountains were barely visible through the cloud cover. It would snow later. Of that he was sure. He urged the horse Austin had loaned him to keep up. "I'll get out of here as soon as I find a place."

No way was he taking advantage of his friend's hospitality.

"What's your rush?" Austin glanced at him. "Afraid I'll work you to death?"

He pulled a face, not bothering to respond. Yesterday, after leaving Ken's office, he'd packed up the weekender, loaded his truck and thoroughly cleaned the place, then tossed the Christmas tree on the brush pile behind the old sheds. As the sun went down, he'd driven off the land he loved. Hadn't even allowed himself to look at the farmhouse on his way out. Too painful. Too raw.

He'd called Austin and said a silent prayer of thanks when his friend insisted he stay there until he figured things out. He didn't think he had it in him to stay at Dandy's Bed and Breakfast. Not when everyone around here knew him and would ask questions, putting their own spin on what had gone wrong.

What *had* gone wrong?

Why was he out of work, out of a home and so confused about Tess he couldn't think straight? Christmas was six days away, and he hadn't felt this lost since the last time he was homeless. That had been a rough time in his life.

Tess was coming home this afternoon. She'd find out Ken had fired him. She'd realize he'd cleared out the cabin without a goodbye. She'd be hurt, angry with him for leaving them in the lurch. Sure, Ken hadn't given him much choice, but if his health took a dive because of Sawyer quitting, she'd blame him for that, too.

"See the ridge over there? Let's check the gully beyond it. There's a couple cows who like to hide there." Austin pointed to his left. Sawyer nodded, and they headed in that direction.

The cold air smacked his face, and he didn't care. Checking cattle with Austin beat sitting around chasing the same old thoughts in his room.

And he'd been chasing them hard. He wanted to talk to Tess. Ached to tell her the truth.

He loved her.

But she wanted to be friends.

If he talked to her, he'd feel guilty and end up going back to the ranch and working part-time for her father for pennies. She wouldn't even have to ask him to. He just would.

He'd hear the worries in her voice, take one look into

her beautiful anxious eyes and he'd take that burden from her. No questions asked.

If he went back, what would it get him?

A lot of heartache. Nothing else.

No thanks.

He didn't hate himself enough to be her dad's servant. And that was exactly what he'd be. A ranch hand who took orders and worked long hours for nothing.

They reached the top of the ridge. No signs of any cows. Just acres of sage brush poking up through the thin layer of snow.

"I think we're good." Austin nodded to him. "Let's head back. Are you sure I can't convince you to work for me? It's good to ride the land with you."

"I'm not working for you. Or any of the other guys." He wouldn't be a burden to them. "I'm getting a job in town."

"In town?" Austin asked. "At least that means you're staying in Sunrise Bend."

"Yeah, I'm home for good."

They spent the next hour taking care of the horses and finishing the chores before going in to get ready for the late-morning service at church.

After showering, Sawyer buttoned his shirt and made a mental list of things to do. This afternoon, he'd look into apartments. Then he'd walk around town to see if there were any help-wanted signs.

The small house outside of town, the quiet life could still happen. It just wouldn't happen the way he'd hoped.

Late Sunday afternoon, Tess set the last of the gifts Devin's parents had given Tucker on the floor of the living room and plopped down on the couch. Her stomach growled, and she pressed her hand to it. *Not yet.* She shouldn't be hungry anyhow. She and Tuck had slept in and eaten piles of pancakes and bacon, then stopped at a Western store to buy Sawyer a present before making the long, lonely drive home. It had helped clear her mind.

As the hours passed, she became convinced Sawyer was the man for her. She had to tell him the truth about her feelings. She didn't want to be just friends. Yes, she was jittery about the thought of dating, but if they took it slow, maybe it would be all right.

It was also time to reinstate Sawyer's pay. She didn't care what she and Daddy had to do to afford it. Sawyer deserved his full salary. She'd pay it herself out of the money she made from her business if necessary.

Ten minutes. She'd rest her eyes for ten minutes. Then she'd find Daddy and lay down the law regarding Sawyer's wages.

"Mama, twac, twac." Tucker climbed onto the couch and pulled on her arm.

"No tractor today, Tuck." She didn't bother opening her eyes. "Tomorrow. Okay, bud?"

"Where Soy?"

"He's out with the cows." Or cleaning up sheds or taking care of the horses or calculating exactly how much hay the cows needed or…

"Where Papa?"

"I don't know. In his room?" She hadn't seen her dad yet. She should check on him. Opening her tired eyes, she sighed. "Come on. Let's find him."

Taking Tucker's hand, she made her way to Daddy's bedroom. The door was open. No one was in there. Last week he'd spent a few hours every afternoon puttering around the ranch. She didn't like that he was ignoring the doctor's orders to take it easy, but when had she ever been able to stop him from doing what he wanted? Besides, having him out there had given her an excuse to avoid Sawyer.

"Papa must be outside."

Tucker let go of her hand and tore down the hallway to the front door. "Me go, Mama."

"Noo." She was not bundling up and going out there. "Mama needs a few minutes to rest."

Thankfully, stomps on the porch alerted her Daddy had returned. He entered the house moments later.

"Papa!" Tuck wrapped his arms around Daddy's legs and grinned up at him.

"Hey, squirt. You're a sight for sore eyes." He looked tired. His face was gray.

"Are you okay, Daddy?" Frowning, she hurried over to take him by the arm. "Come on in here and sit down. I'll get you a cup of coffee."

"I'm fine." He coughed deep and harsh. "A cup of coffee might warm me up, though."

They walked to the kitchen, where he sat on a stool. Tucker dragged his bin of cars over and plunked his bottom on the floor to play with them. Half a pot of coffee was left from the morning. She heated up two mugs in the microwave, then set one in front of him.

"You're overdoing it."

He didn't look up.

"You don't need to be out there. Sawyer has it under control." Something in his posture put her on notice. He was hiding something. "What's going on, Daddy?"

"Nothing to get all worked up about, Tessie-girl."

The hair on her arms rose. "You might as well tell me now. I know something's wrong."

"Nothing's wrong."

If he wanted to play that game…she might as well tell him her thoughts on Sawyer's salary now since it was clear they'd be arguing soon.

"I'm reinstating Sawyer's salary." She raised her hand. "Hear me out. He's worked longer and harder than any cowboy we've had around here. The ranch looks good. Everything's organized. He's cut costs in a lot of places. Enough to pay him what he deserves."

Daddy shook his head.

"It's not up for debate," she said. "I'm adding a Christmas bonus, too."

"And how are you going to do that?" He slammed the mug on the counter, splashing the coffee.

"I don't know yet. But it's the right thing to do."

"Well, you can't."

"And who is going to stop me?" She had a say in the ranch, too. She'd been using her child support payments to cover the groceries, the electricity, Daddy's pain meds. She had every right to make this decision.

"He doesn't work here anymore."

The world seemed to stop spinning. Slowly, she set her mug on the counter and took a step back. "What are you talking about?"

Had Sawyer quit? Had he been offended when she told him they could only be friends?

Of course he'd been offended. What guy wouldn't be? She'd given him mixed signals.

"Look, you said yourself money's tight." Daddy grabbed a napkin and blotted the coffee spill. "And now that Bud quit and I'm feeling better, it makes more sense for me to manage the ranch. I told Sawyer he could stay on part-time. He quit yesterday."

If her face revealed half as much revulsion as her heart was pumping out, she'd be a shoo-in for an extra in a horror flick. She covered her mouth with her hand and shook her head. "No. You didn't."

"Don't act so offended. You should be glad I can run the ranch again. Makes it easier for you to balance the books. You told me the money situation isn't good. I fixed it."

She didn't have words. She simply stared at her father, no longer recognizing the man she knew and loved. Who was this man? How could he be so cruel?

"Don't you dare look at me like that, Tess." He pointed to her. "I did this for you. It's not my fault he quit."

All the times Devin had twisted his actions to justify them came back to mind. They always ended with blaming her.

And now her own father was doing the same.

"You did this for yourself." She turned on her heel. "Leave me out of it."

With her heart beating triple-time, she put on her boots and coat and slammed out the door. She jogged down the porch steps and ran down the lane. Snowflakes swirled around her, but she barely noticed. Didn't stop until she reached Sawyer's cabin.

His truck was gone, but she knocked anyway. Waited a minute. Knocked again.

Left the porch and went over to the window. Curving her hands around her eyes, she peered inside.

It was empty.

Sawyer was gone.

Sawyer shoved his hands in his coat pockets as he walked the sidewalks of Sunrise Bend that afternoon.

The overcast sky would soon give way to dusk. An apartment complex on the edge of town had one vacancy, but he couldn't afford it until he found a job. As for that, he'd yet to see a single help-wanted sign.

How had his life come to this?

Loneliness weighed on him. Sure, he had friends, but he didn't have Tess.

When he was with her, he felt accepted, like he was good enough. And it made him think all those years in New York hadn't been a waste but preparation. For what? He couldn't say. He just knew he didn't feel *less than* when she was around.

Snowflakes started tumbling haphazardly, clinging to the garlands and wreaths strung throughout the town. He tucked his chin into his coat collar. The Christmas decorations would normally cheer him up, but they only underlined his new reality.

He'd fallen in love again. With the wrong girl.

He never should have kissed her. Should have quit on Thanksgiving when she told him they were running out of money. Shouldn't have offered to take the pay cut. Should have seen it coming when Ken demoted him. Why had he trusted the man in the first place?

Had Ken ever planned on retiring? Or had his goal always been to get a strong cowboy to do the work for low pay until he got through treatment and could kick him out?

A gust of wind had him ducking into the recessed entryway of the dentist office. He shivered and tried to clear his head. Instead of clearing it, though, snippets of past Christmases played like a highlight reel through his mind. Of cutting down a Christmas tree with Dad and Mom before she died. Her big smile as they played

Christmas music and decorated the tree afterward. Her joy at singing hymns in church on Christmas morning.

His mom was gone. His dad was gone.

Maybe he should forget about Sunrise Bend. Go back to the city. Get his old job back.

Dread and panic pounded in his chest. No, he couldn't go back. He wasn't meant to live in cramped quarters. Whatever else happened, he belonged in the country, here in Wyoming.

These wide-open spaces were good for his soul.

The urge to call Tess overwhelmed him. He stretched his neck from side to side. *Lord, give me strength. Don't let me repeat the mistakes of my youth.*

The sign for the Barking Squirrel glowed in the glass window across the street. The diner was old-school and had been a staple of the town for as long as Sawyer could remember. He checked both ways and crossed the street. As a bell clanged overhead, he went inside and shook his hat free of snow. Then he approached the counter and took a seat on one of the stools.

A speckled laminate counter and a big board listing the menu faced him. Booths lined the wall and square tables dotted the rest of the room. It smelled like French fries and bacon. His stomach grumbled.

"What can I get ya?" A woman in her fifties with short gray hair and a tired look in her eyes wiped the counter in front of him.

"Is the manager in?"

She shot him a disappointed look. "Rex is off on Sundays."

"Will he be here tomorrow?"

"Ten o'clock."

He debated ordering something, but his phone rang.

Rapping his knuckles on the counter, he nodded and thanked her, then strode out of the diner and took out his phone.

"I hear you're looking for a new place to live." It was Mac.

"Word travels fast." He strode through the falling snow in the direction of his truck parked at the other end of the street.

"You weren't around when my dad went through his big-game hunting phase. Wanted a retreat to bring all his CEO buddies to. He had five cabins built. They used to stay in them for a couple weeks of the year. Anyhow, Dad lost interest and bought condos down in the Bahamas for them to go to, so I'm stuck with empty cabins."

"Look, I appreciate what you're doing, but—"

"But what? I've got empty cabins, and you need a place to stay. I expect you to pay rent." Mac rattled off a number so low Sawyer let out a guffaw. He opened his mouth to refuse, but something held him back.

For years, he'd shut out his friends, refusing to confide in them or trust them. He'd hid in the city, ashamed of himself. And now they wanted to help him out, and he was refusing them again.

But he wasn't ashamed of himself this time. And if the situation were reversed, he'd want to help them, too.

"Double the price and you're on."

Mac took his time before replying. "You haven't seen the cabin yet. You might think the rent's too high."

"It won't be."

"Well, I have the key here if you want to check it over before making a decision."

"I'll stop by right now."

"Great. See you in a few." Mac hung up.

He stared at the phone for several seconds, willing Tess to call.

She wouldn't. He knew why. He'd kissed her, revealing the feelings he had for her that she didn't have for him. And then he'd let her down. He'd left her, her son and the ranch vulnerable.

There would be no happy ending for him this Christmas.

But then, for him there never was.

Chapter Twelve

Her first instinct was to call Sawyer and demand he tell her where he was so she could drive there and talk this out. But she backtracked to the lane, looking—really looking—at the ranch, and her heart had shriveled. The pole barn, where they'd bonded, going back and forth with ideas about the ranch, laughing at Tucker's antics. The stables where they'd kissed. The sheds, once ramshackle, now repaired. Christmas wreaths on every door. Everywhere her gaze landed she saw tidiness where before there had been neglect.

A strangled sound erupted from her throat.

What had she and Daddy done to him?

Clenching her fists, she closed her eyes and stood with her face turned up as the snow came down. Shame spilled down her core. Daddy had treated him so poorly.

She'd been selfish, too.

When Sawyer offered to take the cut in pay, she hadn't cared he'd be working for crumbs. All she'd thought was it would solve some of her problems. It would help Daddy. It might save the ranch.

And then Bud had quit, and Sawyer had been stuck

with all the work. Had she cared? No, because she was too wrapped up in getting her own business started.

And then when Sawyer had held her and comforted her and kissed her—making her feel cherished and important and smart for the first time in ages—she'd set the rules. Said they were friends. Friends only. Because she was too scared to be more.

Daddy wasn't the only one who'd taken advantage of Sawyer. She didn't have to look in the mirror to know she had, too.

It had been her way or nothing. Some friend.

Shame pummeled her. The cold stung her cheeks, so she forced her feet forward. Where had he gone? One of his friends' places, most likely.

How could she fix this? What could she say to make it all better?

She rounded the bend and trudged toward the house. There was no fixing this.

She'd latched on to Sawyer like a leech. Taken from him without giving in return.

He probably hated her, and she didn't blame him.

Neither she nor her father deserved Sawyer. He was better off without them.

Monday morning, Sawyer set the final box down along the living room wall of his cabin on Mac's ranch. He had no intention of ever unpacking. Couldn't do it. Couldn't wrap his head around the fact his days working cattle on the land he loved were over.

Had Ken checked on the small cow who'd had a slight limp last week? Was he riding out to all the hiding spots in the bigger combined pasture?

Why was Sawyer even thinking about it? Wasn't his problem anymore.

He went into the kitchen and opened the fridge he'd stocked earlier. This cabin was nice. Way nicer than anything he'd lived in. According to Mac, the cabins had been built six years ago and barely had any guests. His father had spared no expense. High-end appliances, solid surface countertops, expensive furniture, professional photography mounted and framed on the walls.

He pulled out a Coke, cracked it open and took a long drink.

Didn't feel like home. Not the way the weekender did.

He plodded back to the couch and clicked the remote toward the television. After flipping through channels, he turned it off and reclined back against a throw pillow with his legs stretched out.

Anyone else in his shoes would probably be amped up at renting a luxury cabin so cheaply. Not him. He wasn't a luxury guy. He didn't know what to do with himself in fancy surroundings.

He'd talked to Rex at the Barking Squirrel this morning. Rex hired him as a line cook for the breakfast shift come January third. Then Sawyer would be able to find a more suitable place to rent.

It wasn't his dream job, that was for sure. It wasn't even a job he particularly enjoyed. In New York, he'd had few skills for the environment. There weren't exactly a lot of cattle to raise there.

But here, in Wyoming…

He hauled in a deep breath. Once again, he'd miscalculated. His life hadn't made much sense since leaving Sunrise Bend as a teen, but working with Tess had changed him. Made him see himself in a new light—as a capable rancher.

And now he didn't know what or who he was.

What did he want?

Tess's pretty smile came to mind. And Tucker's arms raised high as he yelled, *Twac, twac!* Riding Pansy across acres of property he still knew like the back of his hand. Fixing shed roofs. Cleaning out the storage room. Logging everything related to each head of cattle to ensure nothing slipped between the cracks.

He loved it all.

But it wasn't his.

A sense of displacement made him woozy, reminding him of the weeks after his father died. All he'd wanted to do was take care of Christina, support her—financially and emotionally. And he'd wanted her to love him, to care about him, to feel the same for him as he did for her. He'd fooled himself into believing she did.

Before he'd driven into Sunrise Bend, he'd been convinced he'd be single forever. He'd been sure any woman he was drawn to would only take advantage of him.

But he'd changed. He didn't want to be single forever. Not anymore.

Tess had trusted him with the ranch. She sacrificed for it, too. Taking care of the books, taking care of her dad, taking care of her son. She was up against an oak of a father, immovable in his decisions, and she'd done the best she could, without much support.

Sawyer had provided a cushion for them both. He wouldn't deny it. And he'd yanked that cushion away, leaving her and the ranch in the lurch.

He sighed. He loved her and Tucker. It would be simple to pick up the phone, call her and apologize.

Simple and fatal.

Which left him right where he was. Renting a luxury cabin as foreign to him as the Upper East Side. He'd be smart to make peace with the fact he'd be spending his days cooking bacon and eggs rather than raising cattle.

His cowboy days were over.

"Tess." Daddy's voice carried. "Come here."

She was not at his beck and call. She stayed right where she was in the laundry room, folding Tucker's clothes. She'd barely said a word to him since Sunday. Here it was, Thursday afternoon, and she had no plans of changing that anytime soon. He was in the wrong. With tomorrow being Christmas Eve, maybe she'd feel more charitable in the morning.

Hacking coughs followed one after the other, and fear set her feet in motion. She tossed the little denim pants on top of the pile and hurried in the direction of the coughs. Her father was doubled over in the hallway, trying to catch his breath. He still wore a hat, heavy winter coat, jeans and boots. The fool was determined to run the ranch by himself.

"Get in here." She put her arm around him and helped him into the kitchen and onto a stool. Then she poured a glass of water and handed it to him. "Drink this."

He obliged, stopping for a sputtering cough. Dark circles smudged his eyes, and his nose and cheeks were red from the cold.

"Are you trying to kill yourself?" She crossed her arms over her chest and glared at him. "You should be in bed."

"I don't need to be in bed." He scowled.

"You can barely stand. I don't know how you're staying in the saddle." Her words were clipped. All week, she'd been so angry she'd refused to think about how Daddy was faring out there on his own. Today, it was obvious he wasn't up to the task. "Take off your coat and let me fix you some chicken soup. Then I want you to rest for a while."

"Soup sounds good." He laid his hat on the counter and slowly took off his coat.

"And then you'll rest."

"Can't. Got to take care of the steers." He coughed into his fist.

"I'll call around about hiring someone part-time." She pulled out the container of chicken soup she'd made yesterday and began ladling some into a saucepan.

"No."

"Just to get through the holidays." Would the man not listen to reason?

"I'm fine. I can do this."

"You couldn't even do it on your lonesome before you got sick. You've always had a couple of cowboys helping out."

"Can't afford it." He wouldn't look her in the eyes.

"That's not true." She stirred the soup, looking back over her shoulder at him. "You have options."

"I'm not selling the land."

"Then cash in—"

"I'm not cashing in anything."

She shut her mouth. What was the point in arguing with him? They'd been round and round this issue for weeks. He wouldn't listen to her. Never had. Why would he start now?

On Sunday, after she'd found Sawyer's cabin empty, she'd gone inside and told Daddy demoting Sawyer was the lowest thing he'd ever done. She'd begged him to change his mind. He'd refused.

And here they were. At the same place they'd been before Sawyer had arrived.

The helpless feeling she'd been fighting her entire adult life reared up like a rattler. She turned her attention to stirring the soup.

Don't think about it. Keep moving forward. You got hired to handle the invoicing for the freight company this morning. Think about that. You're not helpless even if Daddy makes you feel that way.

As soon as the soup began to bubble, she ladled a large portion into a bowl and set it in front of her father. Then she left the room without a word and returned to folding laundry.

She wanted so badly to call Sawyer and ask for his advice. Ask him to help.

But she couldn't.

Sawyer had already had one woman who'd used him. Tess couldn't honestly say she was any better. She'd had no problem with Sawyer working here for next to nothing. He must hate her.

Mac Tolbert's ranch wasn't far. He might have an extra ranch hand he could spare for a couple of weeks.

Would Daddy even let her hire someone?

I am as helpless as I was in my marriage. Voiceless, too.

What she should be doing instead of folding laundry and fighting her father was calling Sawyer and apologizing.

It wouldn't change the situation, though.

"Tess," Daddy bellowed.

Now what? She threw her hands up in exasperation. "What?"

Then she heard a thump on the floor. With her heart beating wildly, she ran to the kitchen. Daddy had fallen off the stool. Crouching next to him, she tried to help him up. "Daddy, are you okay?"

He leaned on her as he struggled to his feet.

"You're going straight to bed while I call the doctor." She helped him hobble down the hall to his room. He sat on the edge of the bed and let her yank off his cowboy boots. As she drew the covers over him, her mind raced with a thousand questions. She kissed his forehead. Felt warm. The thermometer sat on the nightstand along with his medications. Seconds later, the results were in. He had a low fever.

"The steers—"

"I'll call Mac. He'll have someone he can spare."

Daddy lay back with his eyes closed. She pivoted, trying to find the doctor's contact on her phone with shaky fingers. As she made her way down the hallway, a sense of panic gripped her body.

Was this it? Was this the end of her father's life? The fever was low…but it could still turn into pneumonia. The nearest hospital was over an hour away. Should she drive him there?

She dialed the number, and as she waited for someone to answer, she prayed. *Oh, Lord Jesus, please don't take him yet. Please, God, I can't bear it. I love Daddy so much. Please, please get him through this. Don't take him from me. Not now. Not so close to Christmas. Please!*

Chapter Thirteen

"No, Bridget, I haven't unpacked." Sawyer propped his boot on the bottom rail of the corral where Mac's horses were enjoying the sunshine. A thin layer of snow covered the ground. Tomorrow was Christmas Eve, and he'd spent the past few days helping Mac and the other cowboys take care of Tolbert Ranch. Sawyer was amazed at the efficiency of it all. Every time he caught himself thinking about how he could streamline Ken's ranch, he'd get a pit in his gut and remind himself those days were over. "I'm not going to unpack."

"Why not?" Bridget had a direct way of speaking, and she never offered her opinion unless it was asked for. She might be no-nonsense, but she was also compassionate.

"I'll find a place in town when I start working again. You should come out here. You'd like it."

"I know I would." The whir of a coffee grinder flooded the background. "My schedule is crammed, though."

"Work or fun?"

"Fun? What's that?"

He laughed. "I hear you. It'll be strange not celebrating together this year, huh?"

"I'll still get a pizza the day after Christmas and pretend you're here."

"I will, too. We can FaceTime to open presents." He'd sent her a scarf and a photography book featuring coffee.

"I'd like that."

He breathed in the cold air and wished things were different. Wished he still had the job he'd been hired to do for Ken. Wished Bridget weren't so far away so they could keep up their traditions. Wished he had the guts to call Tess and tell her how he felt.

"Are you sure you're doing okay?" she asked.

"Yeah. Why?" He forced an upbeat tone.

"You sound kind of down."

"It didn't work out the way I'd hoped."

"I'm sorry, Sawyer." She hesitated. "You haven't mentioned Tess or Tucker. How does she feel about Ken's decision?"

For weeks, he'd been telling Bridget all about them, including Tucker's cute infatuation with the tractor. He missed the kid. Missed Tess more.

"Haven't seen them. Don't know how she feels." But he could guess. There was no safer person on earth to confide in than Bridget, but something held him back. A cloud passed overhead, dimming the sunshine. He wanted to tell her. Needed to talk about it. "Tess probably hates me."

"She doesn't hate you." Bridget sounded pretty adamant.

"I left without saying goodbye. Abandoned her and the ranch at Christmas while her dad's sick. She has to hate me."

"From what you told me, she doesn't seem the type. Maybe she's upset how everything went down."

"Maybe." He wouldn't put much stock in it, though.

"You don't need to feel guilty about quitting, Sawyer. You and I both know how easy it is to get sucked into other people's problems."

"I know."

"And we've both lost a lot. Do I need to remind you about Dee?"

"As if I could forget." They'd felt sorry for the unemployed woman who'd gotten kicked out of her boyfriend's apartment. Bridget had helped her get a job, given her money to buy food and even let her stay in her apartment. But then Dee stole from her, and Sawyer was the one who'd tossed Dee's belongings into boxes and set them in the hallway, changing the locksets on Bridget's door in the process.

Trust was difficult to give after it was abused.

"You have a big heart, Sawyer. I know I can count on you day or night. If I told you I was in trouble, you'd be here ASAP to help me."

"Why?" His gut clenched. "Is something going on?"

"No," she said with a laugh. "It's just…your loyalty and generosity are what I admire most about you."

"Yeah, well, they can get me into trouble, too." His throat felt scratchy from the emotions her words brought up.

"Is that what you're worried about?" Her voice lilted. "You're not giving yourself enough credit. You're not a teenager anymore. We all make mistakes. We both know I have."

"I don't want to make another one." A gust of cold air made him shiver. He pushed off from the fence and began walking down the lane toward the cabins.

"You got the courage to go back to your hometown

and work on the ranch you grew up on. Ever since you got there, you've sounded happy—really happy."

He didn't have to read between the lines to see where she was going. "You think I should talk to her."

"Only you can make that decision."

"I've been praying, but I haven't known what to do."

"Keep praying. You'll know. I seem to recall you being the one who told me to pray through my problems, oh, about ten times a day when we first met. God loves you. He'll give you peace."

He couldn't help smiling at the memories her words evoked. She'd been young, scared and starving when he'd met her. "Thanks, Bridget. I needed that reminder."

"Well, my break's almost over. Want me to call you later?"

"Nah. I'll call you tomorrow."

They said goodbye and hung up.

His cabin was up ahead, but he backtracked to the stables. Mucking stalls or cleaning up the tack room would keep his hands busy and his brain occupied.

Lord, Bridget's right. You promise peace to those who trust You. I don't have peace right now, and I don't know if it's because I shouldn't have quit or because I shouldn't have left without talking to Tess. I still feel like quitting was my only option.

He had to admit, he felt peace about quitting.

I guess I'm conflicted about Tess. I don't know what to do.

He could leave things the way they were and be miserable. Or he could be honest with her. Tell her he loved her and felt bad about leaving her the way he had, but he wasn't moving back to work for someone who didn't respect him.

I'm scared I'll take one look at her and all my good intentions will fly out the window. I'll feel bad and I'll be too scared to tell her I love her and I'll volunteer to work for Ken and resent them both.

Bridget had said she admired his loyalty and generosity.

Maybe he wasn't giving himself enough credit. Maybe he wasn't giving Tess enough, either. He could have a real conversation with her without caving in to Ken's demands.

Lord, I can't do it without You. Will You help me?

Up ahead, Mac strode out of the stables and waved to him. "Sawyer."

"What's going on?"

"Tess called."

Tess? Had something happened to her? To Tucker?

"Ken's sick. She asked if I could spare a ranch hand."

"I'll go over there right now." His keys were in his pocket.

"I was hoping you'd say that. I'll go with you."

"Are you sure?"

"Ronny can finish up here." Mac held out his key ring. "Drive together?"

"Yeah. Let's go."

Sawyer jogged over to the passenger side of Mac's truck. The ranch, the cattle, Tess—they all needed him. And he'd gladly help out. It was how he was raised. If someone needed help, you put your beefs aside and did what was necessary. He just hoped Ken hadn't pushed himself too hard.

Holding Tucker on her hip, Tess pushed the curtain to the side and craned her neck to look out the window to see if the cowboy Mac was sending over had arrived. The doctor told her to keep her father in bed with plenty of liquids and to bring him in if his temperature got higher. He'd fallen into a restless sleep within minutes of her getting him in bed.

What if this was it? What if Daddy died? She didn't think she could bear it if he died on Christmas.

With a soft sigh, she set Tucker on his feet and lightly bit the corner of her bottom lip. She couldn't bear it if Daddy died at all. She loved him so much. Sure, he was ornery and stubborn and impossible to deal with. But he was also solid and loving. He'd do anything for her and Tucker.

"Moo, moo, Mama." Tucker pointed to the plastic bin of farm animals on the shelf. She pulled it down and set it on the floor. He sat down and dumped all the animals out. Soon he was making mooing sounds as he pretended to make them walk around.

The sound of a vehicle had her looking out the window once more. A truck came into view, and Tess's heartbeat started beating double-time. *Thank You, Jesus*. The Lord had provided in her time of need. Daddy might be ill in bed, but the ranch didn't take sick days.

It had been years since she'd done ranch chores. She could drive the tractor to feed cattle, but she didn't have the experience to know when something was wrong with one of the cows or what all needed to be done on a daily basis.

The sound of two doors shutting reached her. The cowboy must have brought a helper. Good, more hands would make the work go quickly.

Tess hurried over to the front door, not waiting for

a knock to open it. At the sight of Sawyer, her breath caught.

He'd come to help. Even after her father had been so awful to him.

"How is he?" Sawyer's denim-blue eyes gleamed with empathy.

"Resting." She was surprised her voice sounded normal when she wanted to weep with relief. "Low fever."

"That's good. I hope it stays that way. Did Ken mention anything specific needing to be done today?"

"The steers."

Sawyer gave her a firm nod. "We'll take care of it."

She had a million things to say to him, but the most important one got stuck in her throat.

How could she tell him she loved him, she was sorry and she needed him when she was mortified of their treatment of him?

"Soy!" Tucker came running up. Sawyer beamed as he hauled the boy into his arms. Tucker held up a plastic cow. "Moo, moo."

"Nice cow you have there." He ruffled his hair and set him back down. "Destined to be a rancher. Good choice."

"Twac, twac?"

"Not today, buddy."

Tucker's lower lip wobbled and two fat tears dropped one after the other.

"Sawyer's taking care of the cows today, Tuck." Tess picked him up and kissed his cheek.

"Sawyer, I…" She wanted to apologize, but the words got stuck in her throat again.

"I'll let you know when we finish up." He tipped his hat to her, then gestured to Mac to head to the stables.

Tess closed the door and carried Tucker back to his

toys. She sat on the couch as he loaded several sheep, horses and cows into his shirt and brought them over to hop them up and down her legs.

Sawyer had driven here to help. No questions asked. What kind of man did that?

The kind you've always wanted.

She'd wanted to be heard, respected, valued. And after the divorce, she'd convinced herself no man would ever respect her enough to actually listen to her opinion and take her advice.

But Sawyer had proved her wrong, again and again.

Christmas tree lights twinkled in festive beauty before her, and the meaning of the season hit her full force.

She'd never deserved lavish love, but Jesus gave it to her freely. She didn't have to be worthy to be loved and respected.

She already was loved. God loved her so much, He'd sent His Son to save her, and she'd done nothing to deserve it.

She'd gotten the best Christmas gift of all—the promise of eternal life. If Daddy died this Christmas, she'd be devastated. There was no sugarcoating it. But she'd get through it because God wouldn't let her down. He'd hold and comfort her the way He had when Mama died. And again when Devin left her. And again when she'd learned of Daddy's cancer diagnosis.

God had gotten her through it all.

Thank You, Lord. Sawyer showed up today to help and that was the last thing I expected in a thousand years. You keep reminding me I'm not alone. Give me a stronger faith. And please, please, help Daddy get better. Don't take him from me.

Out of shame, she'd convinced herself she didn't deserve to have Sawyer in her life. Kind of like Devin's parents had done with her. Guilt and miscommunication. Both had derailed her relationship with Daniel and Margaret. And both were threatening to derail her relationship with Sawyer.

All because she was afraid. And maybe convincing herself she was unworthy of Sawyer's love was a way of getting out of the hard stuff. It was easier to be silent than to call him, apologize and take another chance on love. Much easier.

Tess let her head rest against the couch cushion.

He deserved an apology from her.

Lord, I'm going to need a lot of help. Give me courage. Give me strength.

If Daddy's temperature held and she apologized to Sawyer, this Christmas might not be a complete disaster after all.

"The ranch looks good, Sawyer." Mac helped him rub down the horses after they'd checked some of the cows. "I helped Ken with branding earlier in the year, and I was surprised at how shabby everything looked. Since you've been back, the difference is night and day."

"Thanks." Sawyer glanced up at him. "I was upset to see it in such bad shape, too. I took it personal. Wanted to shine it up the way my dad would expect."

Mac finished with his horse. "You did good."

"Putting it back in order was kind of like putting myself back in order. I did what I could to get it back on track. It still has a long way to go."

They led the horses to their stalls.

"With Ken being sick and it being so close to Christmas, I'm thinking we should work out a rotation to help out here for the next couple of weeks." Mac followed him outside. "I'll call Austin and Jet."

"That's a good idea." He wished he'd thought of it. "Ken's immune system isn't great. He shouldn't be riding out here in his condition."

"I'll ask Ronny if he wouldn't mind working here mornings instead of my ranch for a while, too," Mac said. "I'll pay him. I don't want Ken or Tess worrying about taking care of the cattle right now."

"That's big of you, Mac." Sawyer frowned. "But don't bother. I'll come over each day to take care of everything. If Tess is okay with it, I'll help here through the holidays. I know what to do. Come January, though, I start my new job. Maybe then the guys could rotate shifts to help Ken out."

It would be Sawyer's Christmas gift to Tess. He'd be doing it as a friend, not an employee. He had free time on his hands anyhow.

"You'd sacrifice your time after how Ken treated you?"

"Yeah." As angry and hurt as Sawyer was, he couldn't hold a grudge against a man fighting cancer. "If it weren't for him, I wouldn't be back here in Sunrise Bend. He gave me the opportunity to reconnect with you guys and give the ranch a boost. My dad would have wanted it this way. He'd want me to help now."

"You're a class act, Sawyer."

No, he was in love. And tomorrow, after he took care of the chores here, he was baring his feelings to Tess. Christmas Eve seemed the right time to have the conversation. No matter what happened, though, he wasn't going to work part-time for Ken. If Tess didn't like his decision, he'd deal with it. If she didn't love him back, he'd deal with that, too.

But he couldn't let things stand as they were.

Sawyer raised his index finger. "Give me a minute to let Tess know I'll be back tomorrow."

"No problem." Mac rubbed his hands together, blowing on them. "I'll get the truck warmed up."

Sawyer strode down the lane to the house. The snowy landscape looked straight out of a children's Christmas book. He knocked on the door. After a few seconds, Tess opened it. The vulnerability in her eyes made him want to crush her to him and take away all her fears and pain. But he awkwardly shifted from one foot to the other.

"I'll be by tomorrow morning to take care of the cattle. I can help out until after the holidays—no charge. Tell Ken not to worry."

"You'd do that?"

"Yeah." He met her gaze. "It's what friends do. They help each other out."

"We'll pay you—"

"No." He shook his head. "I told you—no charge. I'm not taking a penny from you."

"Sawyer…" So many things flitted through her expression, but he couldn't decipher them.

"I start my new job in January, so some of the other ranchers will rotate here while your dad recovers. Mac and I will talk to them if it's okay with you."

She looked stricken, but she nodded.

"I don't want to keep Mac waiting." He hitched his thumb backward.

"Sawyer, I…" She winced, her words trailing off. "We need to talk."

"I know. Tomorrow." He had a lot more to say to her,

but he wasn't saying it smelling like he'd been rolling in cow patties all day. After taking care of the cattle here tomorrow, he'd get cleaned up and return. Then they'd talk.

When he told her he loved her, he was doing it right.

Chapter Fourteen

As soon as Sawyer left, Tess closed the door and didn't move. She'd had oodles of things to say to him, and nothing had come out of her mouth. She couldn't believe he'd shown up to help after everything he'd been through.

Why was she surprised, though? That was the kind of guy Sawyer was. Genuine. Self-sacrificing.

The fact he'd offered to take care of the ranch for free through the holidays so Daddy could recover humbled her. She still hadn't apologized. Neither had her father. And yet…he was generously helping them.

She returned to the living room, where Tucker had curled up on the rug next to Ladybug. She covered him with a blanket, then sat on the couch, staring at the Christmas tree, not really seeing it. Sawyer had mentioned a new job. Was he going to work for one of the local ranches? Or had he decided to do something else? Where was he living now?

He didn't seem to hate her, so that was good.

In fact, he seemed to be at peace.

He was the kind of guy who smoothly adjusted to what life threw at him. Unlike her. She thought of all the moments her stomach had clenched in fear as she dealt with the fallout of her father's rash decisions these past two years. All the times her throat had burned at the risks he took when he was supposed to be taking it easy to get his health stable. All the arguments about the ranch's finances. All the anxiety over if this would be his last Christmas or not.

It was time to let go.

Daddy was an adult. She'd assumed responsibility in areas she had no control over. And when her wishes were trampled, she mopped up the aftermath of his stubbornness. Picked up the pieces time and again.

She did it with Daddy. She'd done it with Devin. And she didn't want to do it anymore.

She wanted the peace Sawyer had, and the solution was simple. She was done picking up the pieces.

Daddy made his own decisions. They weren't hers to make. The consequences weren't her responsibility.

Tess would still be here for him. She'd take care of him. But if he didn't want to pay a ranch hand, that was his choice. If he insisted on riding around the ranch and got pneumonia, it was his choice, too. If he didn't want to sell a parcel of land or cash in one of his assets, he'd have to figure out a way to pay the bills.

Tess wasn't covering for him anymore.

What she'd been doing wasn't helping either of them. The only way he'd make the necessary changes to his life was if he had no other options.

She rose and crept down the hallway to his bedroom. Knocked softly. Peeked in. He was sleeping with his mouth cracked open. She tiptoed inside and felt his forehead. Still warm, but it didn't seem to be getting worse. A good sign.

Halfway to the door, his cough stopped her. "Tess."

"Yes, Daddy?"

"The steers."

"Don't worry." She went to his side. Taking his hand in hers, she squeezed it. "They've been taken care of. Sawyer and Mac stopped by. Everything's okay."

He pushed to sit up, and she helped him, adjusting the pillows behind his back. "Tell Sawyer to—"

"No, Daddy." She kept her voice soft. "He's only helping. He doesn't work here anymore."

He sank back into the pillows.

She sat on the chair next to the bed. "Sawyer offered to take care of the cattle until the New Year. A few of the locals might come out after that. Let your body recover."

"I'll be ready to get back before then."

Still oblivious to reality.

"I can't keep doing this, Daddy." She kept her voice low and soothing.

"What do you mean?" His eyebrows came together as he watched her.

"I've been on pins and needles for months." She gave him a sad smile. "I worry about you. Your health."

"I'll be fine." He nodded as if to assure himself.

"There are more bills than money," she said calmly. "You know it. I know it. I've been using all the child support, and it's still not enough."

"I'll figure it out. I'll take care of you."

"Daddy, we take care of each other, but you don't listen to me. I feel like I'm getting an ulcer trying to keep it all together. So I'm done trying. The ranch, the bills, the decisions—I thought my input mattered to you. But I'm just here for the ride. Nothing I do or say changes your mind."

He stared at her with a confused expression. "I'm in charge. I make the decisions."

"That was all good and fine before you got cancer." Her tenderness for him gripped her heart. She didn't want to have this conversation—not when he was sick, not so close to Christmas—but she had to. She kept her tone soft and gentle. "Like it or not, you won't live forever. And when you're gone, what do you think will happen?"

He opened his mouth, then closed it. His face cleared. "Lots of good cowboys out there who will run it for you."

"And how will I pay them, Daddy?" She wasn't trying to hurt him, but he kept missing important pieces of the puzzle. "I know you don't want to hear this, but the only way I'll be able to keep this ranch going is by selling some of the land *and* cashing in your IRA. And if I can't find a trustworthy cowboy to run it, it won't really matter."

"It's a long way off. Things will change."

"You don't know that." She patted his hand. "Starting January first, I'm going to pay you rent. I'll still run the house, cook the meals and look after you. But I'm done keeping the ranch's books, and I'm not covering ranch costs with the child support anymore."

"Fine." His mouth thinned into a stubborn line.

She sensed he had more to say, so she remained seated.

"Who would you hire to manage the ranch?" He looked at her intensely. "If I died tonight. Who would you hire?"

"Sawyer." She didn't hesitate. "He's a good man. He's done more for this ranch than ten cowboys could. I'd hire him in a heartbeat."

"I see."

"I'm in love with him, Daddy," she whispered.

He seemed to shrink. He looked old. "I'm tired."

She nodded. And left.

It was a start. She was ready to live life on her own terms. Tomorrow, she had to tell Sawyer she loved him. She'd need all the courage she could get.

The next morning, Sawyer zipped through the ranch chores before driving back to his cabin at Mac's for a shower. Wearing his best button-down shirt and jeans along with a pair of clean cowboy boots, he checked himself in the mirror. Not bad.

With a spritz of cologne, he left the bathroom and grabbed his coat along with the gifts he'd purchased for Tess and Tucker. He'd rehearse what he wanted to say to her on the way back to the ranch.

Soon, his truck rolled past the snow-covered prairie. A country version of "All I Want for Christmas Is You" blared from the speakers. Fitting for the moment. Maybe he could croon the song to her and she'd get the hint. As if he'd ever sing. He almost laughed at the thought.

Man, his hands felt sweaty. He wiped one palm down the side of his jeans, then switched hands and wiped the other.

The trip was going too quickly. What was he going to say?

Apologize first. Tell her he loved her. Wait for her to tell him she wasn't interested in him like that.

He gulped. Maybe he should turn around.

No. The look in her eyes yesterday had given him hope she'd be willing to hear him out.

The ranch's drive came into view. He turned and drove up to the house.

This is Your will, right, God? If it isn't, I'll put the truck in Reverse and...

Tess stood in the doorway in a sweater, puffy vest and

jeans. Her hair fluttered around her face, and she brushed it back. Gave Sawyer a little wave.

He cut the engine, got out and took long strides to the porch, stopping a few feet in front of her.

"Hey." He wanted to touch her. Wanted to pull her into his arms and hold her.

"Hey." Her smile made her eyes sparkle. "Daddy's fever broke last night. I think he's going to be okay. And Tucker fell asleep watching a cartoon. Want to take this conversation to the stables?"

"Yeah."

They walked in silence next to each other. When they reached the stables, Sawyer slid open the door and waited for her to enter. He left the door open for light, and Tess sat on a pile of hay bales near the entrance. He sat next to her.

"Sawyer, I'm sorry." She shook her head, all that dark brown hair tumbling around her face. "We treated you badly. I feel terrible."

"Don't." He hadn't expected an apology. "You didn't do anything."

She stared at him like he spoke gibberish. "I let you sacrifice your pay and your time because it made my life easier. And then Daddy took advantage… I was wrong. I never should have used you like that."

The words sorted themselves out in his head, but he still couldn't believe what he was hearing. "You think you used me?"

"I'm no better than your ex-girlfriend." She ducked her chin. "It was wrong of me."

"I offered."

"And I shouldn't have accepted."

"I'm glad you did." His chest expanded. "I needed

this—all of this. I needed to come back here. Needed this ranch. I even needed your dad to demote me."

"How can you say that?" She looked horrified. "He was awful to you. I have no words."

"I needed it so I could figure out what was important to me. And now I know."

The look on her face was pure puzzlement.

"For years, I've been worried I'd be played for a fool again like I'd been played with Christina. I feared I'd willingly give everything away to a woman who wouldn't appreciate it. Someone who would take it all and leave me with nothing."

The color drained from Tess's face.

"I thought I was spineless, and I promised myself I would never fall in love again. I knew I gravitated to the wrong kind of woman."

"I'm so sorry, Sawyer," she whispered.

"And then I met you." He hoped this was coming out right. "You were exactly my type, and it scared me senseless. Then you told me about the ranch's finances, and next thing I know, I'm offering to take a major cut in pay. Same old Sawyer."

She didn't say a word.

"When your dad moved me to part-time, I snapped. Quit on the spot. Moved out that day. And I don't regret it. The only thing I regret is not telling you I was leaving. Can you forgive me?"

"Forgive you?" Her heart had shriveled with every word he'd said, so the concept of him asking her for forgiveness made no sense. "Don't you mean I should be asking you for forgiveness?"

"Why? You didn't do anything."

"Has the snow frozen a key part of your memory? I allowed you to take a cut in pay, watched as you worked night and day to fix this place up, not caring that you were the one making all the sacrifices. I let you do it. I let you because it made everything easier for me."

"That's what friends do." He smiled.

"No, that's not what friends do." She shook her head. This guy was too good to be true, and she had so much hope that she wasn't sure what to do with it. First, she needed to get him to see clearly. "Friends don't take advantage of each other. You've been so good to me, to Daddy, to Tucker. He's obsessed with you. You're more of a father to him than his own dad is."

"How did it go last weekend?" The compassion in his eyes was peppermint drops to her soul.

"It went better than I expected. My ex is who he is, but his daughter is darling. Tuck loved her. And my in-laws apologized to me. They doted on Tucker. I plan on making more of an effort with the family. My little guy deserves it."

"I'm glad." His face was so serene. "You're a good mom, Tess."

It was time to tell him how she felt. The adrenaline pulsing through her veins intensified.

"Sawyer, until you arrived, I was getting through each day. I felt like I had the world on my shoulders. But you drove up and plucked it off like it weighed nothing. And I started leaning on you. You listened to me. Really listened. You didn't brush off my ideas. You confided in me about the ranch, and we made decisions together. It's the first time in my life a man has wanted to work with me and respected me the way you do."

"I'd have to be a fool not to, Tess. You're smart. The smartest woman I know."

No wonder she loved this guy.

"I had a talk with Daddy last night. I told him things are changing around here. I've been trying to hold everything together for him, but he won't let me. So I'm done trying. I told him I'm paying him rent, taking care of him and the house, and that's it. He's going to have to manage the ranch's books and figure out how to pay for everything. I'm done with it."

Sawyer whistled. "How'd he take it?"

"About as good as you'd expect. I'm done wearing myself down trying to manage what I have no control over."

"I know what you mean."

"One thing I do have control over, though, is this." She took his hands in hers. "I want you to know how I feel. I love you. I fell in love with you, Sawyer. I admire you. You're one of a kind. Generous, hardworking—you're the hardest-working guy I know. You make me feel important. And I need you. Not to work on the ranch or to deal with Daddy—although you're great at both—but I need you as my man. I love you. I don't want to do life without you. You're the only man for me."

Sawyer reeled. She loved him? Needed him? Not to ranch but to be her man? Fire roared through his veins, and he shot to his feet, holding his hand out to her. With shy eyes, she took it and stood.

"I love you, too, Tess. I never in a million years thought a smart, beautiful woman like you would give a guy like me a second glance. You're an amazing mom. You give tough love with a gentle touch. I don't deserve you, but I love you. I can guarantee you're the one and only woman for me. Everything I have, everything I am—it's yours."

Her smile was radiant. "Everything I have, everything I am—it's yours, as well. All I want is your love."

"You already have it."

She wound her arms around his neck, stood on tiptoe and kissed him. He held her tightly, amazed at the blessing of her love. He poured all his tenderness for her into his kiss, thankful beyond words this woman was his.

A nicker from one of the horses made him break away. She bit her lower lip and grinned. "That was nice."

"Just nice?" He held her close, staring into her pretty brown eyes shining with love.

"More than nice." Her cheeks were flushed. "Spectacular."

"That's more like it." He kissed her again, reveling in the sweetness of her touch.

Finally, she said, "Come on. Let's go inside."

"I have gifts for you and Tucker." He slung his arm over her shoulders, and she wrapped an arm around his waist. They made their way back to the house as a light snow began to fall.

"I have a gift for you, too," she said. "Do you have plans tonight? I'd love for you to go to church with us."

"I'd like that. If you can believe it, this will be my first Christmas Eve service since I moved away all those years ago. I've always had to work."

"Really?" She leaned closer to him. "I'm glad I get to be the one you spend it with."

"Me, too, Tess." He kissed her temple. "Me, too."

Chapter Fifteen

An hour later, Tess rinsed out the cocoa mugs, her heart overflowing at the sound of Tucker's squeals as Sawyer tickled him. Tucker was smitten with the toy tractor set from Sawyer. He'd only paused from playing with it to gobble a graham cracker. Sawyer had given her a beautiful silver necklace and a mug that said Only the Strongest Women Become Bookkeepers. She, in turn, gave him a rack made of horseshoes to hold his cowboy boots. He'd hugged her tightly and beamed. She couldn't believe how blessed she was.

"Tess?" Daddy called from his room. She'd checked on him earlier, but they hadn't spoken much since last night. She figured it would take some time for him to adjust.

She hurried to his bedroom. "Everything okay, Daddy?"

"Sit down."

She obliged.

"I've been thinking about what you said last night." He had his stern face on. "I never meant for you to feel like I don't listen to you, Tessie-girl. It's hard for an old buck like me to face my mortality. I didn't sell the parcel or cash in an IRA because I want you to have an inheritance besides this ranch. It wasn't because I don't trust you."

His words healed a wound she'd been carrying for far too long.

"I thought I knew best," he said. "I went about it in a way I'm not proud of. I didn't mean for you to worry. That's my job. Worrying about this place is my job. You know that?"

"I do. But in my mind, my job is to worry about you, and the decisions you make about the ranch affect your health."

"I know that now. The good Lord and I had a long conversation last night. That's why I'm putting the ranch in your name. I want you to manage it the way you see fit. Hopefully, I'll be around for a while, but if I'm not, it'll give you a chance to make a go of it without having to sell."

Had she heard him correctly? She blinked rapidly. "I don't know what to say."

"It's time. You've got a good head on your shoulders. I raised a smart girl." He held up his hand. "I'm cashing in the retirement fund. It'll be yours for ranch expenses. No more spending the child support on this place. Save it for the little guy."

Had the earth tilted off-axis? What was happening?

"Daddy, I never meant for you to give me the ranch."

"Well, I always meant to give it to you. Who else would it go to? Why wait until I die?"

"You're sure?"

"I'm sure."

She bent over and hugged him. "I'll make you proud, Daddy. And this ranch needs you. So anytime you're feeling up to it, you keep riding out and doing what you want—those cattle are important to you."

"Thanks, Tessie-girl. Now, do me a favor and send Sawyer in. I heard his voice out there."

Her nerves tightened but she nodded and left the room.

She couldn't believe Daddy was giving her the ranch. He thought she was smart. Tears of joy pressed against the backs of her eyes.

In the living room, Sawyer had Tucker on his lap. The boy was driving the tractor through the air. She perched on the couch arm and wrapped her arm around Sawyer's shoulders. "Daddy wants to see you."

"He does?"

"Yep."

"Well, at least we know he can't fire me." His eyes twinkled as he set Tucker on his feet. "Plow the field while I'm gone, buddy."

Tucker grinned and made chugging sounds as he ran the tractor around the rug. Sawyer held Tess's hand, then kissed her cheek and walked away.

What was Daddy going to say to him?

"You wanted to see me?" Sawyer sat in the chair next to the bed. Ken had the quilt tucked over his lap. He looked tired and old. Worse than he had before Sawyer quit.

Sawyer tapped his fingertips together. If Ken asked him to come back to work to help Tess, he would decline. He didn't doubt himself anymore.

"I owe you an apology, son." Ken looked down at the quilt. "I shouldn't have demoted you. In fact, I'm not proud of how I've treated you at all."

He hadn't been expecting that.

"The fact is I've got blinders on when it comes to this ranch. And when it comes to my daughter."

Sawyer nodded. He understood why.

"I want what's best for both, and it gets me into trouble sometimes. I took advantage of you, and for that I'm sorry."

"I forgive you."

Ken gave him a sharp glance. "You do?"

"Yes."

"I don't have to beg?"

"Nope."

"Why?"

"Because Jesus forgave me for my sins, I can forgive you."

"It's more than I deserve." He seemed to be getting choked up. "Take this." He handed Sawyer an envelope. "Don't open it here. I want to make things right between us."

"You just did."

"I'm making this really right. I owe you money. You're taking it, and there's no argument."

Sawyer accepted the envelope, tapped the edge of it against his thigh. As long as they were clearing the air... "I didn't like the way things ended between us, Ken, but I want you to know how much I appreciate the fact you hired me. You took a chance on me when few would. I didn't know it, but I needed to be back on this ranch. I had a lot of unfinished business in my head about the past."

"What kind of business?" Ken watched him curiously.

"My dad died unexpectedly shortly after I graduated from high school." At the thought of his dad, his throat tightened. It took a few seconds to get himself under control. "Being here, working on the ranch, cleaning it up—well, it was therapeutic."

"It's been a long while since I've felt excited about this place," Ken said. "I love it. Boy, do I love it. But the cancer took more out of me than I cared to admit. And Bud, well, I know he didn't do things right, but I kept him on. Didn't have the energy to train someone else. Then you came and…well, at first I resented you. Made me see how much I'd let this place go. But then I couldn't wait to get out there and see what changes you'd made."

Really? Sawyer hadn't gotten that impression at all. "I'm glad you liked it."

"I was tickled pink when I saw the storage room organized. Took a load off my mind, I tell you. I usually waste half a day trying to find stuff, and now I don't have to."

Sawyer chuckled. "That's why my dad built it the way he did."

"All I gave you was a hard time, but you gave me hope, Sawyer. I didn't even know it until you quit. This week's been tough."

"It's been tough on me, too."

Ken hacked a small cough. "Look, I'm signing the ranch over to Tess. I told her it's hers. She's making the decisions from now on. I think she'll want to hire you as the manager. I hope she does, and this time it will be at full pay."

A nervous sensation fluttered in his stomach. He needed to be honest with Ken. "You made a wise decision. Tess has a good head on her shoulders. And I'm telling you this so we're clear—I'm in love with her. I'd love her no matter what. The ranch has nothing to do with it. If she told me tomorrow she was moving to Maine,

I'd follow her. So if that changes your opinion about me working here, I accept it."

A wide grin spread across Ken's face. "I was hoping you felt that way. You have my blessing. With the ranch. And with my daughter. Welcome back, son."

"Thank you, Ken."

"Oh, and, Sawyer?"

"Yes?"

"Your daddy would be proud of you."

Tears stung the backs of his eyes. He nodded and left the room. Paused a moment after he shut the door. *Thank You, God. I needed to hear that.*

With his heart bursting, he returned to the living room.

"Everything okay?" Tess had changed into a dress and was trying to clip a bow tie on Tucker's collar.

"Everything's great."

"Did Daddy tell you he's putting the ranch in my name?"

"He did."

"Well, my first decision is to hire a cowboy I can trust to run this place." She smiled. "I know you have plans in January. A new job. I understand if you decline, but, Sawyer, this ranch is yours if you change your mind. No one will take care of it the way you do. I'll pay you top dollar if you'll say yes."

"You've got yourself a new manager." He hauled her into his arms and got lost in her sparkling eyes. "I never wanted to be a line cook anyhow."

Her eyes were brighter than the Christmas star topping the tree. He couldn't help himself; he kissed her.

Ladybug sat looking up at them with her tongue out and her tail thumping on the floor.

Tucker ran to them, holding up his tractor. "Twac, twac!"

Sawyer laughed. "Merry Christmas, Tess."

"Merry Christmas, Sawyer."

Epilogue

The icy winds of March froze over half the county, but it hadn't stopped Sawyer from riding out over the land all day. He'd checked the cattle and broken the ice on the surface of their water tanks more than once. Thankfully, none of the pregnant cows were due yet. A couple more weeks and the calving would start. That was why he needed to take advantage of the lull before the long days and nights ahead. Now that he'd finished the chores and showered, he was ready to get this over with.

He was proposing to Tess. Tonight.

Firming his shoulders, he checked his appearance in the mirror. Clean-cut. Nice clothes. He'd have to do.

He'd asked her to come to his cabin—he'd moved back into the weekender on Christmas Day—for supper. Ken was watching Tucker. The man's health had rebounded remarkably in the past few months. He had a lightness, a happiness Sawyer hadn't thought possible. He still went through cycles of cancer treatments, but a lot of mornings he was able to ride out with Sawyer.

They'd relaxed into an easy camaraderie. Understood each other's rhythms. Were on the same page with most of the ranch decisions, including hiring two part-time hands and renting out equipment to cover the costs. And both of them had no problem deferring to Tess for her approval.

Sawyer sent her a quick text.

Want me to bring the UTV over? It's icy.

You wouldn't mind? I've got my cute shoes on.

He grinned. He liked her cute shoes. And her cute smile. Everything about her was cute.

Be there in five.

He slung his arms into a jacket, pocketed the cell phone and did one last check to make sure everything was ready. Two dozen red roses were on the table he'd set with a white tablecloth and fancy place settings he'd borrowed from Mac. A fire crackled in the fireplace, and he had a romantic playlist ready to go.

He patted his pocket. Yep, the box with the ring was still there.

Out in the darkening sky, he braced himself against the wind, jogging to the pole barn for the UTV. It started right up, and he backed it out. Last night he'd met Austin, Randy and Blaine at Mac's house to ask advice about proposing. Jet hadn't been able to come. Even without Jet, four bales of straw would have been more helpful than those doofuses.

It was no wonder all of them were single. Randy had actually suggested putting the ring on the end of a fishing line and pretending to reel her in. Blaine hadn't been any better with his idea. What guy wore camo and took her on a "hunt" for the engagement ring?

Austin had merely shrugged and said to toss it to her and let her figure it out. Mac had flashed both hands near his chest and hissed, "Don't look at me. I'm not getting married."

At least the guys had all wished Sawyer well and promised they'd be the first to congratulate him after Tess said yes.

If Tess said yes…

Sawyer drove down the lane and slowed in front of the farmhouse porch. He left the vehicle running and jogged up the steps. His hand was poised to knock when the door opened and Tess appeared.

His mouth went dry. Her hair had been curled into soft waves, and she wore a long coat over jeans and high heels. Cute shoes, indeed.

He took her arm and carefully led her to the passenger side of the vehicle. Neither spoke on the short ride to his cabin. In no time, he'd whisked her inside, where they both shed their coats.

"You look… Wow." He took both her hands in his and pulled her close. "You take my breath away."

She tipped her head up, scrunching her nose as she smiled. "Why, thank you. You're looking extra handsome tonight, too."

Sawyer's veins seemed to be sputtering.

It was now or never. There was no way he'd be able to get through the meal if he didn't just get this over with.

"This looks cozy." She ambled to the fireplace, turning to face him, and he forgot everything he'd rehearsed. "Cozier than our last date, even."

He'd been inviting her over on Friday nights for supper and a movie. Courting her as well as he could during a brutal Wyoming winter.

"And are those roses?" Her pretty eyes gleamed as she placed her hand over her chest. "My, my. You're romantic."

"They're for you. I wanted tonight to be special."

Her eyelashes fluttered as he drew near her.

"Tess, we've been dating a few months now. I'm more in love with you than I ever thought possible. I'm not getting any younger, and I don't want to waste time." He dropped to one knee, took out the jeweler's box and flipped it open. "Tess Malone, love of my heart, will you do me the honor of becoming my wife? I promise I'll take care of you and Tucker and any other children we have. I'll take care of this ranch as if it were my own. I'll cherish you, because you deserve to be cherished. I'll listen to you, because you're the smartest person I know. And I'll love you with everything I've got. What do you say? Marry me?"

Her eyes filled with tears, but she beamed and nodded. "Yes, oh, Sawyer, yes!"

He rose and fumbled with the ring before sliding it on her finger. Then he brought her hand to his lips and kissed the back of it. She admired the ring for a moment, then met his eyes.

"I love you, too, Sawyer. I want to be your wife. I want to create a life with you here on this ranch, and I'd love more children. I'll cherish you, too."

Pulling her in his arms, he gently caressed her hair, thanking God for the love of this woman. Then he eased back and lowered his mouth to hers. Her lips promised forever, and he kissed her thoroughly, slowly, pouring every ounce of feeling he had for her into it.

When she broke away, her shy smile about did him in.

"Can we have the reception here?" she asked. "We could set up a tent. Invite all our friends."

"A summer wedding?" He could see it. "When are you thinking?"

"As soon as possible. I can't wait to start our new life together."

"I love you, Tess. I can't wait, either."

"Then it's settled. A summer wedding, here at the ranch. Our home."

Home. The prodigal son had returned. And he'd gotten more than he'd ever imagined—a family to treasure.

* * * * *

Look for the next book in Jill Kemerer's Wyoming Ranchers miniseries, coming in January 2022!

Dear Reader,

Welcome to Sunrise Bend, where rugged, loyal cowboys have to fight hard to get what they want, including love. I'm so excited about this new series. Some of you will recognize Hannah Carr from a previous Christmas novella collection, *Western Christmas Wishes*. Expect to see more of Tess's and Sawyer's friends in the upcoming books.

As I was writing this story, my heart went out to Tess and her father. Unfortunately, many people deal with difficulties, including cancer, during the most wonderful time of the year. It's hard not to feel defeated when things are going so horribly wrong. I admire Tess's ability to keep turning to Jesus and to recognize God's love will get us through anything. Whatever you're going through, I pray your eyes turn to Jesus, too. He truly is the reason for the season. You are loved.

I love connecting with readers. Feel free to email me at jill@jillkemerer.com or write me at PO Box 2802, Whitehouse, Ohio, 43571.

God bless you,
Jill Kemerer

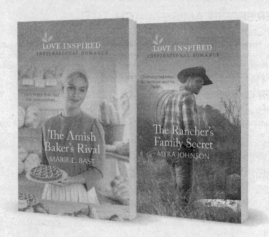

COMING NEXT MONTH FROM
Love Inspired

THE MIDWIFE'S CHRISTMAS WISH
Secret Amish Babies • by Leigh Bale
When Amish midwife Lovina Albrecht finds an abandoned baby in her buggy at Christmas, the bishop assigns her and brooding Jonah Lapp to care for it until the mother's found. But when a temporary arrangement begins to feel like family, can they overcome old hurts to build a future?

HER SECRET AMISH MATCH
by Cathy Liggett
After Hannah Miller loses her dream job, her only option is to become a nanny—and matchmaker—for widower Jake Burkholder, the man who broke her heart when he married her best friend. But as secrets from the past are revealed, Hannah can't help but wonder if *she's* Jake's perfect match.

HER CHRISTMAS DILEMMA
by Brenda Minton
Returning home for the holidays after an attack, Clara Fisher needs a fresh start—and working as a housekeeper for Tucker Church and his teenage niece is the first step. She still has hard choices to make about her future, but Tucker might just help her forget her fears...

THEIR YULETIDE HEALING
Bliss, Texas • by Mindy Obenhaus
Foster mom Rae Girard is determined to give her children the best Christmas they've ever had—and she's shocked when the town scrooge, attorney Cole Heinsohn, offers to pitch in. But after tragedy strikes, could an imperfect holiday be just what they need to bring them all together...forever?

OPENING HIS HOLIDAY HEART
Thunder Ridge • by Renee Ryan
The last thing Casey Evans wants is to be involved in a Christmas contest, but Mayor Sutton Wentworth insists she needs his coffee shop to participate. And when her son draws him into holiday festivities, Casey can't resist the little boy—or his mother. Can they thaw the walls Casey's built around his heart?

A SMALL-TOWN CHRISTMAS CHALLENGE
Widow's Peak Creek • by Susanne Dietze
Selling the historic house she inherited would solve all of Leah Dean's problems—but first, she must work with her co-inheritor, Benton Hunt, to throw one last big Christmas party in the home. Yet as the holidays draw closer, saying goodbye to the house—and each other—might not be that easy.

LOOK FOR THESE AND OTHER LOVE INSPIRED BOOKS WHEREVER BOOKS ARE SOLD, INCLUDING MOST BOOKSTORES, SUPERMARKETS, DISCOUNT STORES AND DRUGSTORES.

LICNM1121

Get 4 FREE REWARDS!

We'll send you 2 FREE Books plus 2 FREE Mystery Gifts.

Love Inspired books feature uplifting stories where faith helps guide you through life's challenges and discover the promise of a new beginning.

FREE Value Over $20

YES! Please send me 2 FREE Love Inspired Romance novels and my 2 FREE mystery gifts (gifts are worth about $10 retail). After receiving them, if I don't wish to receive any more books, I can return the shipping statement marked "cancel." If I don't cancel, I will receive 6 brand-new novels every month and be billed just $5.24 each for the regular-print edition or $5.99 each for the larger-print edition in the U.S., or $5.74 each for the regular-print edition or $6.24 each for the larger-print edition in Canada. That's a savings of at least 13% off the cover price. It's quite a bargain! Shipping and handling is just 50¢ per book in the U.S. and $1.25 per book in Canada.* I understand that accepting the 2 free books and gifts places me under no obligation to buy anything. I can always return a shipment and cancel at any time. The free books and gifts are mine to keep no matter what I decide.

Choose one: ☐ **Love Inspired Romance Regular-Print** (105/305 IDN GNWC)   ☐ **Love Inspired Romance Larger-Print** (122/322 IDN GNWC)

Name (please print)

Address _____ Apt. #

City _____ State/Province _____ Zip/Postal Code

Email: Please check this box ☐ if you would like to receive newsletters and promotional emails from Harlequin Enterprises ULC and its affiliates. You can unsubscribe anytime.

Mail to the **Harlequin Reader Service:**
IN U.S.A.: P.O. Box 1341, Buffalo, NY 14240-8531
IN CANADA: P.O. Box 603, Fort Erie, Ontario L2A 5X3

Want to try 2 free books from another series! Call 1-800-873-8635 or visit www.ReaderService.com.

LIR21R2